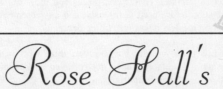

Rose Hall's White Witch:

The Legend of Annie Palmer

LMH PUBLISHING LIMITED

Edited by: Tony Patel
Cover Illustration: Courtney Lloyd Robinson's artistic impression of Annie Palmer
Cover Design by: Sanya Dockery
Typesetting by: Michelle Mitchell

Published by: LMH Publishing Limited
Suite 10 - 11, Sagicor Industrial Park
7 Norman Road
Kingston C.S.O., Jamaica.
Tel: 876-938-0005; 938-0712
Fax: 876-759-8752
Email: lmhbookpublishing@cwjamaica.com
Website: www.lmhpublishing.com

Printed in the U.S.A.   ISBN: 978-976-8245-17-5

Prologue

This book is a version of the well-known legend of the "White Witch of Rose Hall". However, by capturing the intensity of human emotions, the author presents a sincere story strong in universal appeal. The two women, Annie Palmer, the powerful estate owner, and Millie, the free black girl, are caught in the vicious love triangle beset with passion, born of love, jealousy, hatred and disillusionment from the moment both women become aware of the possibility of laying claim to Robert Rutherford, the new English overseer. The story moves swiftly to its inevitable conclusion.

Set in the dreadful environment of a plantation society, the book portrays characters displaying the usual attitude of the heartless and powerful against the helpless and enslaved. However, the main characters, Rutherford, Annie and Millie are treated with unusual sensitivity. As a result, Rutherford contrasts with the other white estate officials in his genuine concern for human beings. Millie is not the usual black girl who has been brainwashed into believing prostituting herself will bring some kind of elevation. Instead, she is a girl genuinely in love and wanting to lead a decent life in the traditions of her tribe. Annie Palmer, under the facade of a wicked witch, wishes fervently to be loved for her own sake and not simply for her power and wealth. The workings of such a plot forms a gripping narrative in which, in spite of the reader's prejudices, his/her deeper feelings are engaged.

Of course, the book, is not wanting in its historical overtones. Plantation slavery is eloquently pictured throughout the narratives. The reader is taken from the cane-field to the mill, to the still-house; from the slave hovels to the overseers' quarters to the Great House. The activities of the slave auction and the wharves, the work of missionaries and the unrest leading to riots are all represented. Superstition runs through the novel adding to the atmosphere of mystery with which Annie Palmer is associated.

The language of the book captures the sensuousness inherent in love stories and also associated with the heady, steaming, lush atmosphere of the tropics. This book recounts the cruelty, inhumanity and shame of slavery. At the same time, however, the reader is saved from feelings of bitterness let alone race-hatred because through Rutherford, we feel that cruelty is tempered with mercy. In the end, though in a most bizarre way, justice is served. As the story closes, there are indications that Annie's spirit will take over now that her body is gone; will there truly be act IV?

Here is a fulfilling addition to any collection of Caribbean literature.

Brief Historical Foreword

The Rose Hall story begins with the sugar plantation called True Friendship (as it was then known). In 1746, Henry Fanning, a bachelor, bought 290 acres of undulating & fertile sugar cane lands, and was married some six months later to a pastor's daughter, Rosa Kelly, but the marriage was short-lived as he died six months later. In 1750, Rosa re-married planter George Ash, who died in 1752.

In 1755, she married her third husband, the Honourable Norwood Witter, who himself died after 13 years. Not to be widowed for long, Rosa married for the fourth time in 1767 to the Custos[1] of St. James, the Honourable *John Palmer*. He was a part of the landed gentry and owned Palmyra, the neighbouring estate and had two sons John & James (Palmer) who lived in England.

It was John & Rosa who built the Rose Hall estate which between 1770 and 1870 became the premier setting for the elites of the then Jamaican society. Rose Hall came to be regarded as the finest residence in Jamaica, with the expansive wide balconies, magnificent carved mahogany staircases, high ornamental arches, Tuscan columns, great chandeliers and the still to be seen broad hewn stone steps, which graced the entrance to today's restored great house. Rose Hall was the greatest of the Great Houses.

For 23 years, John and Rosa shared a happy life until Rosa died in 1790 leaving the entire Rose Hall Estate to her husband.

After Rosa's death, John married the twenty year old Rebecca Ann James, his third wife, in 1792. Some five years later he died leaving both estates in trust for his two sons John and James and their heirs; and, failing this, to the sons of his nephew John Palmer.

Rebecca left Jamaica to live in England and, so, with the absence of Rosa and John and James, Rose Hall passed into the hands John Rose Palmer's grandnephew, John Rose Palmer, who confiscated the property from its absentee landlords.

In 1820, John Rose Palmer married Annie May Patterson, who became the legend we know of today.

Annie May Palmer was beautiful beyond compare; she had a rich throaty voice with black penetrating eyes – locally, they were said to be as black as ackee seeds. Her complexion was smooth and complemented by a small nose and mouth and, at the touch of a button, could shift from a gentle smiling creature to a haughty, cruel, sensual, cat-like woman, gracefully exuding both anger and sensuality. She always basked in the thrill which the reaction to terror imparted to her.

She denied the stories told about her behaviour, as products of gossip, yet, at the same time, she threatened anyone who displeased her with the very form of terror which she disowned. John Palmer did not suspect that any of these things laid beneath the veneer of his beautiful childlike eighteen year old bride, who had come to live in Jamaica in 1818.

Annie believed in sorcery and spirits and displayed no fear of the African slaves' own practice of 'obeah[2].' This all came very easily as Annie had spent all her life in Haiti.

Annie's English mother and Irish merchant father had migrated from the United Kingdom to live in Haiti under an agreement made by King Henry Christophe allowing whites to settle in the then rich and first independent black nation. In Haiti, Annie quickly became the favourite of a voodoo[3] priestess of the highest order in the court of King Christophe[4], and it was she who taught Annie the spiritual world. She took Annie to forbidden voodoo ceremonies where, to the beat of the drum in the dead of night they would worship ancestral spirits and other gods and would summon spirits of black magic and death; and in turn give unto their celebrants the power of a god.

When the priestess died, Annie, whose parents had also passed on, chose Jamaica over England, concluding that the rigid class structure of England was not for her.

John Palmer lived for seven years after his marriage to Annie. During these years, Annie claimed he drank heavily, but not much was said or known of his death and it was only whispered about as Annie would always proclaim that he drank himself to death.

Very little is known of Annie's second husband, who was declared insane, nor of her third husband who, Annie claimed, married her for her money. Like his predecessor he also died under suspicious circumstances. It is said that the room in which he died was closed to only special employees and received no visitors, as the blood stains could not be removed from the floors.

On the other hand, the slaves were fully convinced that poisoning, stabbing and strangulation were the causes of the death of each of Annie's husbands.

This was supplemented by the stories told and by the acts of cruelty carried out by Annie. In one case, she had the head of one of her servants placed in a basket and brought to her after the servant was convicted for his attempt to poison Annie. In another case, Annie had the head of one servant placed on a bamboo stake at Rose Hall and left to decay in the sun for all to see.

It was Annie who gave rise to the fabled 'rolling calf' of Jamaica's folklore; and many have attested to seeing this snorting bull with piercing 'blood red' eyes which brought with it doom and destruction.

The Jamaican medical fraternity could never match or cure the spells of Annie and it was left only to the obeah chieftain to match her guile and cunning.

Annie was a woman of extreme passion, and vanity was her hallmark. She mesmerized the slaves with demonic acts of sensuality and reveled in her ability to weave an air of spiritual mystery and intrigue.

After her three husbands, Annie ruled Rose Hall with overseers and white book keepers, many of them from England and Ireland.

Since most of these white men were usually outcasts and "ne'er-do-wells", she took them on as lovers, indulging their habits whatever it might be – from drinking to cohabiting with the slaves. It was rumoured that Annie could only find satisfaction from the choicest of her slaves, who were favoured by late night calls and visits.

Her sexual desires knew no boundaries and moved from one sexual need to another, be it flagellation or cross-dressing – Annie did it all. One of her favourite acts was to don male clothes and ride through the property whipping the "big buck niggers" into whimpering submission – a dominatrix of the highest order.

Annie was finally murdered in 1831 and buried on the plantation in the East Garden where her grave can still be seen.

Annie's life in the story to follow is set against the changing times of slavery, which was moving from abolition through to manumission and, then, eventually freedom.

The turmoil of Jamaica slave revolts started in the mid 1790's and went on until the mid nineteenth century. Each year, revolts and uprisings increased, and, as a result, the expenses of protecting the plantation owners increased accordingly.

In 1795 the second maroon[6] war broke out when the Trelawny[7] Maroons were publicly whipped by slaves for stealing two pigs – a humiliation that had to be avenged.

In 1798, runaway slaves caused turmoil in lower Trelawny by burning houses, killing settlers and plundering freely. This led to the appointment of a committee of the parish in 1799 to investigate these uprisings which subsided for a few years. From 1805-1809, turmoil reappeared and the year 1808 saw the Fort Augusta[8] mutiny of the second West India Regiment, on which the UK government relied for law and order.

This caused the United Kingdom to withdraw the regiment from active duty, as the government had lost faith in its ability to maintain law and order. And so the escape from plantations increased and 'runaways', as they were called, were estimated to rise to some twenty thousand slaves by 1827. Whipping was the usual punishment for escape, and there is a story of a slave on the North coast who was punished by being ordered to replace a mule on the outrigger and who with the other mules was driven about the property all day.

Written in the *Journal of Occurrence*, on the Rose Hall estate and dated May 27th 1830, one year before Annie's death, is the record of one of Annie's favoured slaves, Hercules. "Hercules, after receiving chastisement for his late desertion escaped once more but on this special night when he was captured, he was handed over to Annie in whose bed chamber he remained." Hercules ran away in two further occasions, but was recaptured and always forgiven, a very unusual act for Annie.

The last recorded mention of Hercules was in November 16th 1830 and states "Hercules after being pardoned for his last offense again made his exit." This was one year before Annie's death.

The year 1831 marks Annie's death and saw the 'Salt Spring Mutiny' which happened shortly before Christmas. It began when the Salt Spring Estate attorney, William Grignon, seeing a woman with a sugar cane in her hand ordered her to be flogged; the order was refused, and not being able to get any slave to respond to his demand, he rode to Montego Bay and reported the matter. Following the report, the police visited the estate where they were faced with the belligerent slaves armed with cutlasses.

Having lost faith in the West India militia and fearing further developments, and seeking to ease the panic that was developing, the governor sought help from the missionaries to pacify the situation; the missionaries led by Henry Bleby[9] appealed to the slaves to return peacefully and quietly to work, which they refused to do.

The situation became even more intense and the appeal from the missionaries to wait patiently on the Lord for deliverance was, as history records, rejected and Rose Hall was burnt to the ground during which Annie Palmer herself was murdered.

---

1 The principal magistrate of a Parish, appointed by the governor-general who is the queen's representative; the name and office are derived from the Latin *Custos Rotulorum* ("Keeper of Rolls"). In earlier times, before representative government, the custos would have presided over the vestry – the local government which managed the affairs of the parish. The importance of the office was much greater in the past, today, it is largely ceremonial.

2 In Jamaican parlance, it is used to denote witchcraft, evil magic or sorcery by which supernatural power is invoked to achieve personal protection or the destruction of enemies. It is also used to describe any non-Christian beliefs, practices and rituals.

3 The practice of sorcery in Haiti is referred to voodoo. It refers to the summoning of supernatural powers to inflict harm or protect individuals.

4 Christophe, Henri (1767-1820), Haitian president (1807-1811) and king (1811-1820), born on the island of Grenada. After fighting at Savannah, Georgia, during the American

Revolution, Christophe went to the French Caribbean colony of Saint-Domingue (now Haiti), where he joined with black insurgents fighting against the French in 1790 and became one of their leaders.

5 Legendary calf-like monster-animal with red, fiery eyes, trailing a clanking chain and capable of growing to huge size, rolling over and over as it moves around the countryside at nights.

6 Africans who escaped from enslavement in the New World and set up their own communities throughout the Americas fighting to retain their freedom. Unconquered, Jamaica's Maroons eventually forced the British colonial authorities to negotiate peace treaties that gave them their own land and some internal autonomy in their settlements.

7 Formed in 1770 from the Eastern portion of St. James after the wealthy sugar planters of the coast complained that the town of Montego Bay was too far for them to conduct business. The parish was named after Sir William Trelawny, who was governor at the time it was formed.

8 Now a prison for women, it was formerly a fort guarding the western end of Kingston Harbour.

9 Henry Bleby, the Methodist pastor who ministered in Falmouth at the time of the Sam Sharpe Rebellion in 1831. He was also actively involved in the movement for the abolition of slavery.

Chapter 1

The shipboard life over the nine months that Robert Rutherford had spent travelling from London to the Islands, and indeed his earlier life in Bristol did not prepare him for the sight of the high mountains which formed the picturesque backdrop to the city of Montego Bay. Truth be told, however, he anxiously looked forward to the feel of solid earth under his feet.

He could not help but be impressed by the beauty of the Jamaican north coast line — its pristine white sands being gently caressed by the frothing waves, whose intensity as they approached the shore would be cooled and broken by the natural coral reefs which protected the Northern shores of the island.

It was early morning as the ship glided into the deeper end of the port, parting the glistening waves, which reflected the morning sun in sliver-like shivers.

In the port could be seen two other merchant ships, from whose belly had just been spewed the raucous unmannered dragooned outcasts, men or sailors if you wished, who had been hurriedly ganged into service, men of many nations and, equally, of many pasts. Rutherford watched as they now mixed with the off duty red-coated dragoons. In the distance, as he descended the steps, Rutherford could see a 'Gibbet' from which still hung the corpse of an unruly slave. The harshness of the sight was jarring to the unaccustomed eyes of Rutherford and starkly contrasted with the earlier beauty he had witnessed.

In contrast to the motley scene of sailors and dragoons, were the well-dressed merchants, obediently trailed by their slaves, some of whom were loaded with their owners' wares, and were themselves interspersed by freed Negroes, not unnoticeably dressed in the cast off clothing of their former masters. Intermittently scattering them to either side of the road were the splendid carriages of the local gentry as they overtook and sped past the heavily laden oxen carts carrying barrels of rum to the port — rum to satisfy the belly of the ship, and create greater wealth for the absentee landlords, who lived in splendid isolation in England and Scotland, occasionally sending their offspring to the Islands, as family outcasts, no longer wanted or needed in England.

This was the commerce that the abolitionists wanted so much to ruin, for what could replace the trade between West Africa and the British Ports of Liverpool or Bristol, if they were not allowed to sell their manufactured goods to West Africa and use some of those profits to buy and sell their slaves to the West Indies. Indeed, it was their ability to pack the holds of the ships beyond capacity that would ensure the 100% profit and more, and which, when unloaded in the Caribbean, would carry back the cargo of rum, sugar, indigo and other produce, returning much profit to the attorneys, drapers, grocers and barbers whose returnings financed these voyages.

It was now mid-morning and at the other end of the street, George Baxter sat in his book-lined office, going through his limited appointments for the day. He was a man of corpulent proportions, who despite his weight and his age of fifty-five, had kept pretty active, more so because he consistently had to visit the surrounding estates as far as Falmouth which was some thirty miles from Montego Bay, and lay over a wandering dusty road which took almost a day to traverse.

Clustered around the verandahs of the houses and the offices, as mute witnesses to this repeated daily scene, were the petty-traders' wives, women of the freed slaves who had come to set up their stalls to cry out and sell their wares. In the distance, a lonely Negro sang a

2

blend of spiritual hymns; he was middle aged with a face that reflected the years of servitude. But his eyes still looked with questioning vision to the future — an unclear future. It was the period between abolition of slavery and manumission — the period when slaves were able to buy their freedom without much awareness of what the future held for them.

The planters were also holding meetings across the island to protest the impending doom. Rutherford had no real feelings on the matter. He recalled that the British Parliament had promulgated a new policy for the amelioration of slavery which would have led to the natural extinction of the system.

One of the splendid carriages pulled up to the solidly built two-storied buildings, surrounded by a verandah with fully grilled trellis work, just as Rutherford arrived and noted the sign which identified the office to be that of C. Baxter, Lawyer and Minister of Law.

Baxter's office formed part of the street, which framed the busy little port and was itself lined with one or two other elaborate two storied buildings, buildings with widely overlong eaves, which offered shade to the verandahs which lay below.

Rutherford stepped up to the verandah, at the same time that the carriage itself pulled up. He was a tall white man of exceptional good looks, and his aquiline features carried with it an air of authority. In England, he had indeed been known for his charm and 'good breeding', but what was equally noticeable about him was his pale skin tone, which revealed him to all as one who had just arrived to the sunny island. Equally betraying his newness was the cut of his clothes, which bore the unmistakably tailored look of the English gentry.

He entered the office of George Baxter, moving from the excessive heat of the street, to an office cooled by a large fan suspended from the ceiling — a fan which he noticed was operated by a small Negro boy, some eight or nine years old, who quite ungraciously rotated the fan by a series of strings and pulleys sometimes using his hands and sometimes his feet.

Rutherford was paying both courtesy and business calls on the Jamaican family lawyer, whom he had been advised by his father in

Bristol 'to seek out' immediately upon his arrival in Jamaica — and for whom he carried a letter of introduction.

"Good morning sir. Is Mr. Baxter in office?" he enquired of the wizened clerk sitting at the desk outside the glass-panelled door. Wordlessly, he was ushered into Baxter's office. He watched as Baxter lifted his eyes from a mounting pile of nail clippings and peelings, which he caringly and carefully husbanded before him on the blotter of his desk. The clerk completed his duties when he pulled out a chair for Rutherford and wordlessly withdrew. Rutherford cleared his throat and offered a polite good morning to Baxter, who paused momentarily as he reached across the desk to hand him the letter which would explain his presence.

After opening the letter and reading it, Baxter glanced back down, and without again looking up said, "My boy, would you take me into your confidence and tell me what on earth would prompt you to leave your home in Bristol so precipituously, to come to this the end of the world and to be an overseer, no less! You can trust me; was it women or gambling debts?"

The question asked by Baxter drew no passion from Rutherford, as he was fully aware of the custom of British families, especially the land owning gentry, to send their sons, their ne'er-do-wells, to the Island. Baxter himself had come to this conclusion when he received the unexpected advice from Rutherford's father, for whom he had legally acted for many years, when he was seeking to buy land in the Caribbean.

Smilingly, Robert replied, "Drink! And how to make money from it." The reply forced Baxter to look up at Rutherford, who, clearing his throat, went on, "My father wished me to spend some time learning the business of running a large sugar estate plantation on someone else's land, where I would be regarded as a worker and not be overly favoured as the owner's son."

A disappointed Baxter began to scrape up his clippings, realizing that his attempts at eliciting gossip had brought him no further to knowledge, than what he already knew. Not being happy at his failure, he added, "I will tell you my boy, if we were in court I would seek to get more out of you. However, good manners does not permit me to call the son of an old friend and client a liar."

As both looked into each other's eyes, they discovered a liking for each other, and almost as an afterthought, Baxter added, "I hope it wasn't drink; for rum plays the devil with you young fellows out here in the hot sun of the islands". In an almost similar afterthought, Rutherford assured him that it wasn't drink "You see Mr. Baxter, my father has recently purchased an estate in Barbados and as earlier stated, he felt it would be better for me and the estate's future if I learnt the business from the bottom up — so to speak, and on someone else's estate."

Smilingly, Baxter shouted to his wordless clerk, Joseph, to have his servant, Felix, bring drinks of cool lemonade for him and 'Massa Rutherford'; while he began to carefully gather up his filings. Rutherford watched curiously as he set about the task of gathering up the parings of his fingernails, which he carefully rolled in a piece of blotting paper, and placed in an ashtray on his desk. Rutherford watched enquiringly as he opened a box of Swan matches and set fire to the parings with a single match.

Noticing the care and intensity that Baxter applied to the task, which in London would have been a simple task of throwing the particles into the nearest bin, he felt compelled to comment. Baxter, without taking his eyes off the ashtray and still concentrating on the burning particles replied, "Well my boy, you are certainly not in England. Even then, were it the age of witchcraft in our own country, you too would be careful of what you do and when and where you do it. Please remember that you will never do that here in Jamaica, for these are living particles of your body, and here you never leave these particles and yourself wide open, to be tampered with and used against you in obeah practices. Remember those natives are still just out of the Jungles of Africa."

"And what may I enquire is Obeah?"

Realizing now that Obeah meant nothing to Rutherford, Baxter repeated with emphasis, "Voodoo — witchcraft! Obeah my boy is the serious practice of voodoo and witchcraft which is carried out daily by the slaves of this country and is no laughing matter to those who have witnessed its workings and suffered at its hands." Not being sure if his host was pulling his legs, Rutherford treated the discourse with noticeable amusement, which forced Baxter to continue, more seriously and with great sincerity. "This island, young man, is full of obeah — it's the root of much of the trouble here. That and the namby-pamby abolition talk in England."

Rutherford was aware of the growing cry in England ever since William Wilberforce had decreed his objections to slavery saying, God Almighty has set before me two great objects: 'The suppression of the slave trade' and 'The Reformation of Manners', this he further recalled, had led to the ruling by Lord Mansfield Chief Justice of England in the Granville Sharp Suit, which led to the freeing of slaves in the British Isles in 1772.

Baxter continued, "I must not weary you with our local politics, as you will need to leave for Rose Hall." And with that Baxter rose from his well-worn leather chair, extending his self-manicured hand to bid Rutherford good day. "If you do not mind, Sir," said Rutherford, "I would like to stay in Montego Bay a day or two, and get the feel of the town."

"Not at all, Rutherford! You are most welcome, but I fancy they are expecting you at Rose Hall, and the owners of Rose Hall are not persons who like to be kept waiting. I know they are hard pressed to complete the cutting of the sugar crop and they are shorthanded, with the slaves in a truculent and rebellious mood."

"I am afraid they have to wait, as I am increasingly aware that a book-keeper's role is not one of immense pleasure, and I will need a horse, or a carriage like the one I saw outside."

Knowingly, Baxter looked at Rutherford, and felt it incumbent on him to remind him, "You know Rutherford, mules are usually provided for the overseers of Rose Hall". He listened as Rutherford replied, "I prefer horses, and it's one of the few things I know something about, and I certainly do not intend to ride such stubborn animals as mules." But not wishing to take the matter any further, he felt he would let the young man discover some things for himself, for after all, was life for the young not more enjoyable when they experienced the pitfalls themselves? And somehow, he felt that Rutherford would not be deterred from his own ideas of his needs and desires.

"In which case Rutherford, you can see what you can find at the auction being held just down the street, and Felix can take you there if you wish." With that done, Baxter took hold of his young visitor and guided him out of the office unto the verandah, where he instructed Felix to accompany him to the auction.

Moving into the heat of the day created beads on Rutherford's brow. Felix with great agility guided him to the auction. Rutherford arrived at what was, to his unaccustomed eye, a most remarkable sight; as there before him he confronted a raised platform made of wood which took up some twenty square feet, in front of a house quite like the one occupied by Baxter's office. Standing before the platform was a cluster of what he presumed were planters and overseers, and at a further distance, as was their custom, stood a group of mostly Negroes, who had, or so he thought, come to view the proceedings, out of mere curiosity.

On the platform was a man of immense size who almost filled one quarter of the platform. He wore a broad hat and carried a serious scowl on his equally broad face, marked with the line of constant exposure to the heat of the Caribbean sun. His broad nostrils were panting from the exhausting heat. Rutherford watched, as the man whom he now knew to be the Auctioneer, disdainfully turned to his clerk and ordered him, "Bring out the next animal".

The clerk in turn beckoned to the Negro groom to bring the horse forward. Rutherford immediately took a liking to the horse, which he saw was a mare, and as his experienced eye wandered over the neck and the forelock, he sensed that there was some spirit in the animal.

"Fifty guineas," boomed the voice of the Auctioneer, "fifty-five, sixty, sixty-five," as he sought to move the bidding along.

"What did you say Sir?" Rutherford thought how much different this was from auctions in England.

The bid of sixty-five had come from the front of the auction and from where he stood, Rutherford could not at first see who the bidder was, but he watched as the Auctioneer looked toward a large, weather beaten and heavily-muscled, sharp-featured white man dressed in working clothes but carrying an air of authority. "Come Mr. Ashman, an animal such as this is worth more than that!" The Auctioneer glanced up, and his eyes caught Rutherford who immediately nodded in his direction and listened as the Auctioneer shouted, "Eighty - I am bid, thank you Sir," and turning back to Ashman he said, "Mr. Ashman?" After a slight hesitation, Ashman nodded, and the Auctioneer shouted, "Eighty-five?"

He switched his looks back to Rutherford who unhesitatingly upped his bid to ninety. At the same time, he noticed that the man, now referred to as Ashman, was now staring coldly in his direction.

The Auctioneer, looking intently at Ashman, questioned of him, "Ninety-five, Mr. Ashman?" but receiving no response he went on to complete the bid for the third time and intimated the horse as sold to Rutherford, who could not help but notice the look of anger on the face of his opponent bidder. "And you sir! If you will give your name to the clerk, he will settle the matter with you." He signalled to the clerk to move to the next order of business.

Rutherford felt a slight charge move through the audience as he moved forward to supply the clerk with the details of himself as requested by the Auctioneer.

Responding to a new signal from the clerk, Rutherford watched fascinated, if not uncomfortably so, as a bunch of six Negro girls were pushed on to the platform. He could not help but notice how their hands were fettered. They were accompanied by a slave driver, who stood mercilessly with whip in hand and ready.

"Lot 60!" shouted the Auctioneer. "Six Mandingo female slaves, in excellent condition, prime stock straight from the coast of Guinea, still virginal and straight from the hold of the Vera Cruz which only arrived this morning." His nasal impassionate voice carried with it a ring of disdain.

The slave driver dragged the first girl forward, roughly raising her arms above her head - almost simultaneously lifting her tattered smock above her shoulders to cover her head. Rutherford noticed that she wore a string of beads around her sinewy and shapely hips, which was covered by a narrow 'shame' cloth. The driver spun her around to display her to the crowd; despite her obvious thinness, Rutherford could not help but notice that there was something appealing about her.

But witnessing this his first slave auction was very disturbing to his genteel upbringing. The insulting behaviour of the crowd, as they responded in equal manner as they did to the auctioning of his horse, was one he found difficult to accept. He felt even more angered as the slave driver with one hand, pushed the girl's head between her legs while he kept her knees stiff. It was at this juncture that he allowed some of the planters, especially those nearest to the girl, to pinch her legs and thighs and indeed one or two of the planters themselves got on the platform to examine her, as they would sheep for the market.

Rutherford watched, quite dismayed, as one of the planters signalled to the driver to rip off the girl's shame cloth, whereafter he lifted up the girl's leg and began to squeeze her inner thighs. At the same time, the driver opened the girl's mouth and showed it to the planter, who peered in. Rutherford could only but wince when the slave driver gave out for all to hear — "See Sir, no sores on her at all."

"A prize piece of nigger, gentlemen," shouted the Auctioneer. "Unbroken, no sores, a little thin, but will soon fatten up. A good strong female to work and breed from — I call her Dawn."

Rutherford was now more than taken aback by this, his first sight of a slave auction, and his reddened features stood out in marked contrast to the rather bored looks of the planters, who, it was clear to him, were more than accustomed to such auctions. "Who will start the bidding?" shouted the Auctioneer, "Who will start me off at four hundred? Four hundred from the Busha at Cinnamon Hill, may I say four-fifty — come gentlemen, six perfect females. "One of the planters standing nearest turned to Ashman and expressed surprise — he was not bidding — "We no longer have time at Rose Hall to break in new raw niggers, and as a policy, we breed from stock," was his measured reply.

All eyes focussed on the platform. Very few, if anyone was interested in what was happening elsewhere and almost unnoticed except for Rutherford, among the Negroes, and standing to the side, was a tall well built Negro. Rutherford guessed he was somewhere in his late fifties, his strong black face and stature, were carried with a great deal of authority, and he was better dressed than the other freed Negroes around him. What kept Rutherford focussed on him was his recognition of a smouldering look of anger on his face.

Rutherford's reverie was disturbed by the hammer of the Auctioneer as it slammed on the pedestal and the six females were led off, sold for four hundred guineas. The females were now replaced by the clerk, with a single, tall, well built Negro, who breathed an air of truculence and insolence.

"Lot 61," shouted the Auctioneer, "Aaron the Fantee, a strong buck nigger, being sold here today on the instructions of Mr. Rockford of Fairfield. Come gentlemen, and look at the splendid specimen, strong as an ox — a most precious field hand." The slave looked arrogantly around him, catching the eyes of the other freed slave who Rutherford had first noticed. By this time, Rutherford had enquired of Felix who the Negro was, and had been given only his name reluctantly, "Him name Takoo."

Rutherford could see his anger now in check, how Takoo sought to give the man Aaron courage. "What am I bid," shouted the Auctioneer — "one-fifty?" seeing that there was no response, he shouted, "One-twenty-five" — at this precise moment the man called Ashman moved forward to look at the Negro and the Auctioneer, and in a voice full of challenge he bid ten pounds. A tremor ran through the crowd, accompanied by a buzz of voices and scattered laughter, "Come on Mr. Ashman, a Fantee nigger like this? I cannot accept ten pounds."

In almost one swift movement, Ashman pushed his way contemptuously forward and leapt onto the platform and spun the Negro to the crowd, lifting up his shirt to reveal Aaron's back, which was marked with numerous lacerations, some old, some new. Turning to the crowd and for the Auctioneer's benefit, he reiterated his knowledge and history of the slave, Aaron, whom he accused of attacking the owner of Fairfield and nearly slitting his throat.

10

The Auctioneer, flustered, began to stutter, as Ashman challengingly turned to the crowd and in his loudest voice, said, "Any advance of ten pounds." Nobody stirred; the planter nearest to Rutherford was heard by him to remark to his companion. "You know it is much wiser for one to put them down once they are wild as he is, but Ashman is the only one I know who can handle cattle like that."

Once again the Auctioneer's hammer descended to break the tension as Ashman grabbed the ear of the slave, with one hand, and with the other hand forced him to his knees. "No tricks with me boy!" The slave glanced at Ashman defiantly. Ashman responded with a slap of the back of his hand while twisting his ear. The slave grimaced with pain, but retained the look of defiance; as he replied, "Yes, Massa."

Ashman pushed Aaron to the floor, leaving it to the driver to push the slave to his feet and hustle him towards the Baracoons He departed the platform, pausing only to respond to the Auctioneer clerk who had enquired, if he wished for the slave to be branded there and then, or would he wait till he took him to Rose Hall, and carry out the branding there. "Do it here," Ashman hurriedly replied.

His reply was lost however to Rutherford, who was distracted by the singing approaching in the distance. The sound drew closer and louder, prompting the Auctioneer to look up with annoyance as it would now most certainly interfere with his day's work. The planters began to show irritation and were becoming restless. Rutherford watched intently as the band of marchers joined their voices which had preceded their arrival. At the head of the procession, was missionary the Rev. John McPherson, a tall reedy English man of the Methodist religion. He was accompanied by his wife, who was equally tall, but an obviously shy Welsh lady; behind them was a band of some six young coloured children, all singing the protest poem of John Cooper, which Rutherford had listened to on numerous occasions while at home — it was the rallying cry in England for the freeing of the slaves.

The Methodists had since 1831 established their work in Jamaica and had spread their wings across the island seeking to convert the slaves, for which they faced great hostility from the planters who all but advocated lynching of the preachers.

The Auctioneer, intent on carrying on his work, ignored their arrival and continued his auction, and Rutherford watched as the planters laughed derisively at the missionary.

Rutherford watched as the missionary reached for a crate belonging to one of the petty traders who was now about to protest. The Reverend proceeded to climb up on the crate and harangue the crowd about the evils of slavery and the slave auction. He spoke of its debilitating effect on the dignity of man. "Dearly beloved, friends, slavery crushes the human spirit, degrades the slaves and the slave owner, and belongs to the dark ages. In the name of God we must end it."

There was much amusement at these remarks, but Rutherford noticed that there was a tension building in Ashman, who now carried a serious look and stood glaring at the Rev. McPherson. Not being able to control himself any longer, Ashman charged through the crowd and kicked the crate from under the missionary, who fell sprawling in the dust. Unable to stand by and watch any further, Rutherford shouldered his way through the crowd and placed himself between a rather surprised Ashman and the preacher whom he proceeded to help to his feet. Ignoring Ashman, he helped to dust the Rev, off, and turning to the rather embarrassed preacher, he enquired, "Do you wish to continue your sermon?" But the missionary, noticing the intense anger of the crowd, decided that for this time, discretion would be the better part of valour, and advised Rutherford that he had finished his sermon. He took hold of his wife's hand, and, with his small procession, turned and headed back to the centre of the town.

To the majority of planters and slave owners, these missionaries were considered dangerous meddlers and their activities in educating slaves and giving them status in the Church underminded the social system and the economic well-being of the estates.

As the pastor withdrew, a loud response emanated from the chorus of planters accusing the missionary of inciting a rebellion and failing to understand the way of plantation life, and the economic needs of the plantations. Further angered, Ashman made a great effort to control his temper, which was heightened further by the rude indifference of Rutherford, and with a look of scorn on his face, he turned to

Rutherford and meaningly enquired, "You are not a plantation owner, are you?"

Rutherford recognizing the need to stand his ground, replied, "Nor am I an abolitionist or a bully, but if you wish to know who I am, then lawyer Baxter can so advise you."

His courage in standing his ground and the firm resolve in his voice eased the tension. Ashman laughed, but with obvious contempt in his voice, spoke loudly to the crowd, "God deliver us, a gentleman, all the way from England by his looks, and one who will need a bit of education in our island. You had better understand, sir, that we don't like tampering with our property, and it will do you well to remember that our business is growing cane and shipping rum. You would do well to mind your own business, or take yourself and your do good companion back to England." Ashman turned brusquely away, leaving Rutherford with little doubt that any further meeting between them both would not end quite as peacefully.

"Brand my slave now!" he demanded as he moved away from Rutherford, who watched him as he walked away. He himself was not able to conceal a wince.

He watched as Ashman moved out to witness the branding of Aaron, his newly bought slave. He watched as Aaron was tied to a pole and the branding iron singed his shoulder with the initials R.H., the same as was on the rum barrels. The smell of the burning flesh assailed the nostrils of Rutherford, and the initials stood out on the singed flesh of Aaron, whose features of antagonism and defiance never changed. Somehow, Rutherford felt that in that look Aaron was sending a message, that in time his turn would come.

Rutherford watched intently as Ashman loaded his cart with rum barrels and slaves, both branded alike, and with the crack of the whip sounding in Rutherford's ears, drove off towards the end of the street.

Rutherford, deep in reflection as to what his future here would be, turned and walked back towards Baxter's office. This, his first introduction to plantation life, was in itself most disturbing to him, but did not seriously dampen his resolve to fulfil his father's wishes.

On his arrival back at Baxter's office, he met him just leaving for his home and accompanied him to his place of abode for the night. Baxter could see in his manner and his silence a change in his approach to Island plantation life, which was obviously more problematic than he thought of while in England. No doubt the problem was due to the vacuum being created by the lapse of time between manumission and abolition, the latter being fought against by the plantation owners, who demanded compensation for their loss of slaves.

He expressed some of these concerns to Baxter, who sought to guide him in his approach to the situation. Over a light dinner, they examined the possibilities of what lay ahead, finally deciding that it would be unwise for Rutherford to stay any longer than overnight and to leave early the following day for Rose Hall.

In his discourse with Baxter, not wanting to worry him in any way, he intentionally left out the confrontation with Ashman and the whole encounter with the preacher.

This did not prevent them from sharing thoughts on the developing situation of the British Parliament's new policy and approach for the amelioration of slavery, recommending such things as the abolition of Sunday market, the prohibition of the flogging of female slaves and admitting slave evidence into court. All of this was questioned by the crown colonies, and more so by the self governing colonies like Jamaica, who took the strongest exception to the measures and questioned the right of the British Parliament to interfere in a purely internal matter.

Chapter 2

Rose Hall

The following morning Rutherford rose early. He had slept only fitfully, unaccustomed as he was to the island days and the island noises. He had gone to bed to the sound of the whistling toads and barking dogs, and woke to find that this was complemented by the crowing of the cock in the distance. He rose and watched the early morning sunlight move the leaves of the trees to dew-like tears. On his emergence for breakfast, Baxter guessed at his feelings, and perhaps his forebodings, but thought it better to leave him to his own thoughts.

His decision was to travel to his destination as early as possible and so he saw to the preparation of his newly bought mare, which, as he expected, did indeed have some spirit. He made final enquiries of Baxter of the direction to the plantation, and found himself reacting with much apprehension and anticipation, not unmindful of the quite unusual and unexpected happenings of the day just past. Bristol now seemed so far away.

Rutherford bade Baxter goodbye and mounted for his ride to Rose Hall, carrying with him a great feeling of premonition that he was on his way to an experience that would stay with him for the rest of his life.

He moved out on the main street and followed the route which Baxter had told him would take him to the imposing iron gates of the Rose Hall Estate.

His ride was long and dusty, but was most impressive and educative, especially for one eager to learn the way of plantation life. He saw fields of sugar cane on either side of the road, and the expanse of green fields was perhaps the most impressive sight he had ever seen. He watched as the fairy-like cane fronds swayed gently in the breeze. As he rode between the fields, he noticed the slaves cutting the cane and watched as the sun took its toll on the sweating bodies glistening in the morning sun. In some areas, he saw the women collecting the cane and loading it on to the ox-drawn carts which waited in the 'intervals' running between the fields. Behind these women were children he later learnt were called 'picaninny gangs'. Their job was to see to the cleaning up of the cut cane sections to ensure that no possible piece that could be used to produce 'King Sugar', would be left uncollected. At the farther distance behind them were Negro women each with a switch ensuring that the children gangs would not dawdle or idle away the time.

He noticed with great alarm how the structure worked, as not sitting far away, under the shade of a guango tree, were some twenty or thirty slave babies, toddlers, who were watched over by an old woman, while their mothers carried out their field tasks of either loading the cane or controlling the picaninny gangs.

Not unnoticeably, standing out from this sea of bodies, but dominating the gang of working slaves, were the overseers, who in almost every case appeared to be half caste (mulattoes); they stood out, if for no other reason than that, additionally they were mounted on mules, with guns fixed in their belts and the ever present whips at the ready.

It was clear to Rutherford, that the slaves, without breaking rhythm, would glance surreptitiously at him. But his eyes were more and more overwhelmed by the sheer beauty of the estate. He now approached the great house, which stood imposingly on a slight rise of land at the end of a palm bordered pathway whose fingers pointed the way to the great house.

Rutherford could not help but be impressed. Even by the highest English standards, the house which he now approached would be considered opulent, a fulfilling complement to the estate as a whole. The lawn and shrubs of a well kept garden surrounded the house, and a few gardeners could be seen tending the flowers which grew in profusion, interspersed with bougainvillea and night jasmine. As he glanced, he noticed the broad, hewn, wide stone steps which led to an elegant portico, framed by a pond. But it was the palladian colonial façade of the imposing stone - built great house that overwhelmed his attention as he pulled up his horse before the portico.

Rutherford dismounted as one of the gardeners came up to take the reins of his horse. He ascended the stairs to the immense double doors and pulled the bell cord to announce his presence. He immediately noticed the initials R.H carved in the frame of the door. The sight of the initials reproduced in exactly the design as that on the barrels of rum and on the slave Aaron once again gave him the uneasy feeling of foreboding and made him vividly recall all the happenings of the previous day. As he turned and looked into the distance, while awaiting the response to his pull of the bell cord, he was almost breathless at the beauty of the fields of cane stretching into the distance reaching out to caress the blue azure sea, and blending with the tropical sky and the glistening rays of the morning sun.

It was truly a glorious vista of a fecund land, a land seemingly at peace with itself, somewhat disturbed only by the sweat glistening off the backs of the slave gangs working in the distant fields, as it imposed its tax on the human body, taking its toll by the drawing of sweat and blood.

Acres of cane field stretched before the eyes, and Rutherford could just see in the distance a small cluster of barracks and low houses which he almost instantaneously knew housed the field slaves. This was perhaps because he had quickly become accustomed to the contrast between the owner and the chattel as played in his introduction to the life of the island, and his ride to the Great House.

He was startled out of his reverie by the unlocking of the great mahogany doors, which were opened by an elderly house slave, from whom he enquired the whereabouts of the manager. Before the slave was able to answer, Rutherford heard the thundering sound of horses' hooves on the stone paved courtyard, and found himself all but ignored, as a maid rushed past and hastened down the stairs to greet the new arrivals.

Rutherford himself turned to look at the two arriving persons who had now pulled up sharply and dismounted. He was somewhat startled, but not unduly surprised, as he had earlier come to recognize the brand R.H. Immediately, he recognized one of the riders, the man, as the planter, with whom he had exchanged words yesterday at the auction, and who was now giving instructions to one of the slaves, with his back turned to Rutherford.

Rutherford paid little attention to him, however, as he was completely overwhelmed by the sheer beauty of the woman who was ascending the stairs. Her smooth black hair, small but sharp nose and a mouth with gentle child-like smile touching the corners of her face, could now be clearly noticed by Rutherford, and, as she came closer, he could not help but be mesmerized by her black, penetrating eyes, which he held in an intense stare, feeling almost as if his soul was bare. All but overwhelmed by the pressure of this beauty before him, he bowed low, hat in hand, and blurted out almost mischievously, "Ma'am – your slave."

Annie was flushed after her ride, and small beads of sweat caressed her forehead; her well cut riding habit showed off her slim figure and with the chemistry of the moment generating unseen but felt tensions, they both took a long measured look at each other, immediately recognizing the electric fascination.

After what seemed like an eternity, Rutherford broke the charge that had built up between them, and with some urbanity remarked, "I swear ma'am, I am more than overwhelmed by the beauty of it all," and with that he moved his hand in a wide sweep, to indicate the vista of the Rose Hall Estate, "such glory, such translucent beauty, and more so complimented by the grace and beauty of yourself." His effusiveness was obviously spontaneous and Annie reacted to it with unexpected enthusiasm.

She looked at him, with her eyes taking him all in; in her rich melodious voice replied, "I do declare sir, the sight of my few acres have often inspired people to envy, but very rarely to poetry. You do not live here, do you sir?"

Rutherford's thoughts were still scattered; events were unfolding rapidly and he knew he had to set about the business which had brought him to Rose Hall.

"Robert Rutherford, Ma'am," he replied, still a little shaken by her beauty. "I have come to pay my respects to your mother and trust it is a convenient time." Amused by it all, Annie could not hold back her reply, "I will convey them to her sir, although she has been dead for some twenty years." Rutherford could not help but notice the mischievous smile which played around her eyes and embarrassingly begged her pardon. He proceeded to advise Annie that he was indeed her new book-keeper. "I understand arrangements have been made for my arrival."

It was now Annie's turn to be a little confused, as she had never been accustomed to book-keepers of Rutherford's class and breeding, for the levels of the plantation society bred strong social and class barriers. As his words trailed off, Rutherford heard the ascending footsteps of the man who had ridden in with Annie, and as he turned away from Annie, both their faces registered instant recognition. Facing the man whom he now recalled was called Ashman, Rutherford could see on Ashman's face even more than he knew existed on his own. Acting out his surprise, Ashman shouted, "By God! The abolitionist, straight from England."

Rutherford returned his face to Annie and looked to see what her response might be. He immediately saw that it was obvious that Ashman had relayed his run in with him at the auction to Annie. At the time of the telling of the story, Annie could not see any humour in it at all, but now as she saw the two men together she immediately realized that Rutherford was so much unlike the usual run of the mill book-keepers that she and Rose Hall had been accustomed to, and one that was way beyond the ability of Ashman to handle.

Rutherford, not sure what to expect, was a little mesmerized by the event. He was however happily surprised when Annie burst into happy laughter, a laughter which carried for Rutherford's ears the peal of deep sensuality, "So you are the man that caused all that turmoil in town? Really Mr. Rutherford, you should not go around Jamaica attacking and antagonizing my Estate Manager! Those things are just not done you know." Before Rutherford could reply, Ashman angrily interrupted and questioned Rutherford's presumption to call directly at the house, "Your instructions, Sir, were to report to my office, and above all I want my book-keepers to obey orders! And get rid of that horse. Rose Hall book-keepers ride mules." Rutherford realized that Ashman was seeking to stamp his complete authority on the situation and to send a message to both himself and Annie, rather less than to get even with the incident at the auction.

But he was not about to back down from the challenge, and so drew himself up to his full height and without losing his composure and noting the amused smile on Annie's face, felt a tinge of his own mischief was needed to complement the mood of Annie, and so replied, "But horses are so much more stylish and suitable, Mr. Ashman, and I shall be glad to pay for its upkeep, if that, Sir, is your main problem." He watched as Annie, with an amused laugh, turned to Ashman, and slowly but with new emphasis said to Ashman, "I think Rose Hall can afford the fodder for Mr. Rutherford's nag, Mr. Ashman, and you will now have one more mule to spare."

Rutherford could not help but notice the sour look which came over Ashman's face, as without any response to Annie, he called one of his slaves to take Rutherford to the book-keepers quarters. Turning back to Rutherford he coldly bid him goodbye, seeking to sound as mannerly as he could, as he advised him to go to the quarters and report to Burbridge, the senior book-keeper. "And we do work here at Rose Hall, Rutherford. This is not the place for sissies and ne'er do wells so as of now start following orders, and don't step out of line."

Deciding to continue with the mischief of the moment, Rutherford looked him straight in the eyes and mockingly retorted, "You know you amaze me, Sir," and with an ironic bow to Ashman, and a parting smile to Annie, he said, "But then Rose Hall has been full of delightful surprises." With a chivalrous bow to Annie, he went down the stairs, smiling to himself, fully satisfied that the morning's escapade had now prepared him to face the rigours of Rose Hall Estate life.

Annie watched with undisguised interest as he followed the servant and jumped on his horse, with the slave preparing to run before him; almost tauntingly she turned to Ashman and was heard to remark, mischievously, if not teasingly, "I must say he has a good seat on a horse. I think he will be an asset to Rose Hall."

Ashman, slow as he was to grasp the subtle innuendoes which passed between Annie and Rutherford, could not help but realise that the situation was already taking the wrong course, at least for him, and found himself responding with a great deal of passion.

"The man is soft, coming here and seeking to flaunt his airs and graces and full of insolence." Annie, still in her mischievous mode, with a smile, moved up the stairs and with a parting shot said, "You should have thought of that before you brought him here, Mr. Ashman." Accompanied by her house maid who had stood silently aside watching, she entered the cool foyer of Rose Hall Great House.

Chapter 3

The Early Days

$\mathcal{F}$ollowing the slave who never broke stride in leading the way to the Barracks, Rutherford arrived at the low, unpainted shack, which was by now bleached from years of exposure to the intense Caribbean sun. His eyes took in the small narrow verandah which ran along the front and the back of the building. He noticed two half caste girls, seemingly arguing with each other, under a shady guango tree which stood not far from what Rutherford felt was the kitchen and the wash house. As he approached, he could see that the women were haggling over some fish, and he could see that the lighter complexioned of the two had a degree of pride and spirit which matched her attractive face. She stood out in contrast to her other companion, who was loudly protesting the price she was being asked to pay for the fish. Their argument trailed off as they saw Rutherford arrive, and one of the book-keepers, came out of the shack to greet him. The guide slave, as was his custom, proceeded to the house to announce to Burbridge the arrival of the new bookkeeper.

Rutherford observed that Burbridge could not be much out of his twenties, and despite his obvious youthfulness, he looked tired, and was clean but shabbily dressed. He was obviously glad to receive a new companion, and expressed this in his most noticeable north country accent.

"We've been awaiting your arrival. It's the worst time of the year. We are shorthanded and I don't believe Ryder or myself have had four hours sleep in the last two weeks." Rutherford sensed that the person he was referring to was the other book-keeper who shared the house with them.

"It's nice to know I am welcome. It makes a pleasant change after Mr. Ashman."

"Ay – he would not be happy with your late arrival and on a horse no less, and you would be well-minded to keep on his right side. For once you lose your job on this rum-soaked island, it's hard to find another." Still talking, he led Rutherford into the house, but not before he had introduced the two female combatants he had earlier seen, as Millie and Psyche, both of whom, out of curiosity had drawn near, listening to the exchange between Burbridge and himself before they moved inside the house. As she moved, Psyche could be heard, "Ay – because a you Miss Millie, me never tidy up Massa room." She hurriedly disappeared in a flap to the back of the house. Millie ignored the remarks of Psyche, and with a show of arrogance stooped down and picked up the load of fish, which she placed on her head with the grace of a princess, and moved past the window through which she could see the two men talking.

Rutherford, on entry from the verandah could not help immediately noticing that the furniture in the house was simply functional: the sitting room, which he first entered, was tidy and clean, and showed very little reflection or personalization of the inhabitants; it represented what it had become over the years of use — a merely impersonal, interim stop, for persons escaping from a past, with little interest or hope for a future. He was startled out of his reverie, by the jarring north country accent of Burbridge.

"We share this the living room and over here behind it is the dining room, and the doors from it, as you can see, lead to the front and back verandahs and also to the bedrooms which are on either side of the lounge." He then led Robert over to the door on the right of the lounge and opened it "This is where I kip," he said. Robert noticed that the room contained a bed, and a wash stand. He also noticed Psyche who could be seen in the room guiltily tidying it up. He could not help but notice the nails on the wall which served as the hangers for Burbridge's clothes; but more interestingly and curious to him was the fact that there were female garments hanging beside Burbridge's clothes.

As if reading his mind, Burbridge turning to Rutherford, said, "And this is Psyche who looks after me as you might say! Psyche, this is the new master." Psyche turned and gave Rutherford a small curtsy — "Welcome Massa." Rutherford sensed the meaning, even though it came over him slowly. Burbridge crossed the lounge and escorted Rutherford to the opposite room, advising him, as he expected, "And this is your room."

The room was identical to Burbridge's only seemingly awaiting the personal identity of Rutherford's belongings. Burbridge ordered Psyche to get some bedding from the store for Rutherford and reminded her to hurry as he reprimanded her for lingering with Millie and noting that she was well behind in her work. He explained to Rutherford the need to get his own helper as was the custom and further remarked, "Psyche can look after you till we find someone for you personally."

Immediately on hearing this, Psyche turned to Burbridge and remarked, "My cousin Calliope, she fine girl for Massa Rutherford, Massa sir."

Rutherford began to fear the course the discussion was taking and began to feel he recognised that there were undertones to the meaning of this discussion, "Surely, one girl can look after both of us?" he said.

"Massa my cousin is pretty girl. You will like her, and both of us could keep the place nice and we both could be happy and virtuous."

"We'll see."

In this exchange, Rutherford learnt that there was an acceptance by the system and the slaves that all the white overseers were expected to take and use the female slaves as they wished — to protest would bring punishment.

Rutherford was taken aback by this last remark, which seemed quite normal for Burbridge and Psyche but it was becoming increasingly clear to him that the exchange of service carried with it more than the mere connotation of house cleaning.

Before Rutherford was able to respond, he heard the door open from the front verandah and a voice gave out, "And virtue is the vale of tears," Rutherford turned to the unrecognised voice. It was the voice of the other book-keeper, Ryder. He was a much older man than Burbridge, in his late forties, with a thin and reedy look, and clothes that hung on his rather skeletal frame in a haphazard and unappealing manner; but noticeably to Rutherford, his speech carried an educated ring to it. Immediately, Rutherford concluded that Ryder was a self-deprecated man, and he could not help but see that he carried an air of defeat with him. He would later on learn that he was in reality, a gentleman, but one who by his past experiences throughout time would carry his defeatism with him, and would let it colour everything he said or did.

He moved forward and took the outstretched hand of Rutherford as he greeted him, and as if taking charge of the situation and knowing the ritual. He turned and sent Psyche to fetch Calliope, her cousin, without heeding any of the protestations from Burbridge and Rutherford.

"Ryder is the name, Sir. Your companion in exile. I would commiserate with you on your new found situation, but latterly I have been saddled with far too much work — so welcome, dear fellow, welcome." Rutherford found himself immediately drawn to Ryder, and concluded that unlike Burbridge he was not taking the bookkeeping job as the end-all of his life.

Burbridge had by this taken out his large timepiece from his pocket and glancing at it with concern, said, "I was about to send for you Ryder, and now that I'm late, will you show Rutherford around and make sure I see you both before Rutherford goes on duty? No reason we should not all get on well together." Finding this comment strange and uncalled for, Rutherford could only reply though with a question on his mind, "No reason at all."

Seeing Rutherford's embarrassment, Ryder said, "You don't look like a bookkeeper." Somewhat irritated by this infrequent observation, Rutherford half laughingly asked, "People keep telling me this. What does a book-keeper look like, Mr. Ryder?"

"They come in two sizes, the young ones who know no better, the old ones who do, and can do nothing else, and those young ones like Burbridge who over time become like Ashman. "What brought you here?" Rutherford warmed to the down to earth approach of Ryder and replied, "Five pounds a month and board."

Undaunted by the remark, Ryder replied, "Oh! And what of anonymity and the access to free drinks, the only advantages of an exiled Englishman? Come now Rutherford, let me guide you around our Kingdom."

Ryder led Rutherford into the sunlight to mount their waiting animals. Ryder would lead him in the direction of the sugar mill and the boiler house to find Burbridge and to receive the further instructions from him.

Ryder led him along the 'interval' which passed between the two closest cane fields and followed the direct path which took them into the yard of the mill and the boiler house. Rutherford handed the reins of his horse to the slave standing under the tree, as they dismounted and walked over to the boiler house which stood in the centre of the courtyard. Rutherford was ushered through the door and immediately reacted to the deafening clatter of the metal rollers as they entered the dark grim boiler house, lit only by flames from the open furnaces, all having been built with little regard for the convenience of the slave workers.

Rutherford watched intently as a group of slaves wearing only loin cloths sweated while they fed the open furnaces with wood; others pushed the cane into the rollers, which crushed the cane and extracted the juice which poured out through the guttering into a series of large cauldrons raised off the floor, beneath which fires burnt furiously and for which the constant cries for "wood — more wood" were heard.

He turned back his eyes which wandered to the great rollers which were run by steam from the open furnaces, and watched intently as other slaves, with long ladles, would skim off the pungent liquor from the cauldrons or 'taches'. He noticed that the thick substance in the cauldrons would constantly bubble and fling up constant explosions of a boiling spray. Hovering over these cauldrons were other slaves who sweated even more profusely than the other slaves. Above them all was the mulatto foreman who would occasionally crack his whip, and rap out the order, "Skim!"

Rutherford wondered how he could ever get accustomed to what he could only describe as a raging inferno of heat, noise and fumes which overpowered the voice of Ryder as he tried to explain the operation to him, who himself being unable to take it any longer held him by the arm and led him out into the yard.

As they stood there mopping their brows, Ryder was the first to speak. "In a day or two you will get used to the noise and the heat, and it will be a comfort to know you don't have to stay inside all day."

"I am amazed that the Negroes can stand it," said Rutherford.

"Don't you know Rutherford, that they only put slaves in there who are worthless and unsaleable, those who have all but served their useful lives; makes sense, doesn't it? Squeeze the last drop out of the cattle before they die off."

Rutherford's face assumed a puzzled look, not really being sure if Ryder was serious. He was about to react with concern and astonishment at this conclusion, when their attention was diverted by the loud arrival of an ox-drawn cart, which proceeded by them. The cart was loaded with puncheons of rum and moved slowly with its cargo of valuable stock, which, Ryder informed him was being taken to the storage room where it would be marked, tagged and allowed to begin its fermentation life.

Noting Rutherford's interest, and wishing to involve him more in what went on at Rose Hall, Ryder guided Rutherford away from the boiler house and down the path leading to the still house. Rutherford could see between a cluster of trees a series of shacks which he opined served for the slaves. Nearby, he could see a small patch of ground which Ryder explained yielded the precious food of cassava and yam, an obvious staple of the slaves.

The absence of life in the field and the silence of the hour was deafening to his ears and contrasted sharply with the noise of the boiler house. The only noticeable exception were the two old women he saw cooking over their outdoor fires, and from whose cooking pots the smoke hung lazily in the midday air.

Ryder continued the guided tour, explaining to Rutherford the details of sugar as a sensitive crop, which had to be cut when it was ripe, not a day before, not a day too late, and twice per year at that. "At which times we and Burbridge would work non-stop and you" — he turned to Rutherford — "could not have chosen a more disagreeable time to come to the island, as we are in the throes of the crop, and we are shorthanded." As they moved nearer to the still house, they passed some of the slave huts. As they drew near to the boiler house, passing through the surrounding huts, Rutherford could not help but notice a grim-like, clay carving, not unlike an 'Ibo' carving, which he remembered from a visit he made some time ago in England to a museum. The carving was set between some of the huts, and protected by a small umbrella-like grass roof. The idol-like figure was surrounded by a mass of bloody feathers, chicken bones, animal skulls and empty gourds. In front of the idol hung a dead chicken with its throat cut slowly decomposing in the sun.

Ryder could see the reaction of Rutherford, and was forced to say, "Lares and Penates, household gods from the jungle of Africa." Remembering the Methodist persuasion and his band of Negro worshippers, Rutherford was moved to ask, "I am amazed the missionary doesn't object."

"You will find out, Sir, that Rose Hall is a very special place and that missionaries are not made to feel very welcome." Despite finding this a strange comment, Rutherford chose to ignore it. As they walked towards it Rutherford seemed to sense an air of reverence on the part of Ryder. "And now let me introduce you to the holy of holies." And with that they both entered the dim large room, along the side of which Rutherford saw standing, barrels upon barrels of puncheons of rum.

In the middle of the room, were vats into which the newly brought cane juice taken from the boiler house was poured, and which after maturation would be drawn out and put into puncheons, always under the watchful eye of the overseer.

It was from here that the slaves would seek to take off what undiluted rum they could, for personal use, the drinking of which could lead to fights and all kinds of happenings, not the least of which would be the attempt to become a runaway slave.

The clatter of machinery from the still house was not unlike the mill, and made it difficult for anyone to hear, and, once again, Rutherford sought the escape of the open air.

As they emerged back into the sunlight, he was startled by the piercing sound of a blown conch shell, which Ryder explained was his call to duty, and which was a call for a complete shift change. Rutherford watched as the slaves poured out of the still house, chattering with relief and rushing towards the barracoons. He was bid good day by Ryder, who headed to the still house and by those who had departed from the still room, so that the endless cycle of production would continue into midnight.

The slaves and mulatto overseers made way for Rutherford who was unable to make out what they were saying, as he set out on his own to return to the house.

Rutherford was a little concerned at what he had seen and as he rode through the slave residence was conscious of the group of slaves squatting on the ground eating with their fingers from round communal bowls. He could not help but notice that this was being done under the watchful eye of an overseer.

As he arrived, weary from his earlier long ride, he dismounted and strode purposefully down the path to his house, past the other outhouse, and past a group of slaves who glowered at him, but continued their eating.

A slave day would begin at four in the morning by either the ringing of a bell by the lead driver, the cracking of the whip, or by the blowing of a conch shell. These alarms would first require 'before day' jobs to be carried out. This could involve carrying mould to the cattle pens, cutting up the dung, making mortar, or carrying white lime to do various odd jobs on the estate, and after this it was off to the fields with hoes and machetes and any late slave would be whipped.

It was work until ten o'clock when breakfast brought by the slave from his house was eaten. At twelve o'clock, the horn equally announced lunch which lasted for two hours, with warning signals at half hour intervals, and following which work went on until six thirty or seven p.m., at which time a roll call was then taken and the slaves sent home. Any malingering would lead to whippings which would be carried out by the slave being stripped, laid out flat on the ground, held down when necessary, and whipped till blood was seen — brine might be added to the wound.

Slave owners were to provide food for their slaves, but most did this by providing land for the slaves on which they were to cultivate their own provisions. Many slaves developed little 'kitchen gardens' around their huts, in which they grew vegetables of all sorts. In addition, the smarter ones reared chickens, goats and cows, but this was only done at the consent of the slave owner as the laws of the country forbade this ownership.

He did especially notice among them, Aaron the slave, whom he had earlier witnessed being sold to Ashman. As he looked through the corner of his eye, he saw Aaron turn and say something to his neighbour, but from the distance he was unable to hear what was said.

He arrived at the house at the same time as his boxes and valises arrived from town, and could not help but notice that Psyche was in a towering rage.

If indeed he had arrived earlier, he would have heard Psyche telling Millie how Takoo had interfered in her plans and was seeking to prevent Calliope from taking up the offer of working for the new white man. "Calliope is be my cousin, and if this white man like her he will buy her free — yuh see Millie, yuh nuh belong to Rose Hall — so what you want to be the new poor book-keeper's woman for?"

"Cause Takoo seh so,"said Millie calmly. Psyche becoming more agitated at seeing her plans frustrated replied very furiously, "Is lie you lie, is tief yuh want tief him, I nuh care too damn much for yuh grandfather Takoo, for he be ignorant nigger, like wi – for choosing a housekeeper is nuh obeah business – yuh fi tell Takoo dat."

Psyche looked up to see this strange look coming over Millie and looked mesmerised with fear as Millie closed her eyes and stretched out her hands.

"Wha' yuh doing Millie," Psyche shouted, her eyes widening with fright as Millie's face went rigid and she chanted,

"Mu prade, mare ba petro Ja petro chen ki chen."

Psyche reacted with even more fear as Millie kept repeating the words which ended with, "Takoo will be punish yuh, yuh insult Takoo granddaughter."

Psyche's eyes became even more filled with fear as she sank to her knees in the traditional tribal way, and grasped Millie's ankles, almost incoherently blabbering, "A sorry, a sorry." Millie fully aware of her fear, placed her foot on Psyche's shoulder, pressing her face into the ground, while she stripped off her sandals using it to beat Psyche on her fat rump.

In the midst of administering the reprimand, not only psychologically but also physically, and despite the screams of Psyche, they both heard the conch shell echo in the distance, and responding to that, looked up to see Rutherford approaching the house. Almost as if by magic, Millie shed her regal poise and once more assumed the role of the mischievous young girl.

Rutherford, unaware of all that went on between the girls, entered the room and greeted Burbridge who was sipping a glass of pure white rum.

Picking up one of his boxes he moved to his room, muttering almost as if merely wanting to say something, "About time I change into something more comfortable," he said.

Burbridge nodded at him as he passed and moved into his bedroom.

As he spoke, he saw the somewhat confused look on Rutherford's face, and felt compelled to add "Whenever any of Psyche's tribe lets her down they always dun die, don't they girl?" And with that said he slapped Psyche affectionately on her behind, drawing an angry squeal from Psyche who sped from the room, her dignity and pride obviously wounded and her behind still stinging from both Millie's earlier beating and the additional pain caused by Burbridge's slap.

"What the matter with the girl?" Burbridge asked, quizzically, and turning to Robert, added, "Don't worry, however, I'll find someone."

Rutherford, without thinking, nodded and walked toward the door, only pausing when Burbridge shouted, "Hey! Rutherford, you've forgotten something." Rutherford turned and looked at him questioningly as he lifted up his hands, in which rested the trademark of all the overseers and the book-keepers, and which he had noticed was standard equipment. Burbridge handed the whip to him, cautioning, "Don't ever go out without it."

Rutherford looked at the whip and felt rather foolish, fully realizing that this was a normal response when one held a slave whip in his hand for the first time; and so whip in hand he strode into the encompassing dusk.

Rutherford's route took him past Ryder's makeshift accommodation, and saw him sitting on the low verandah with a bottle before him and a glass in hand. He recalled Baxter's words and wondered fleetingly if this could ever become his outlet for boredom, as displayed by both his co-workers. "Care for a drink, before you wield your badge of office?"

"No thank you, Ryder, not just now," was his rather off-hand reply.

Ryder rose somewhat unsteadily to his feet, stuttering, "You force a man to drink in solitude?" He shakily caught up with Robert, taking him by the arm as he joined him in his walk along the foot path towards the still house, where he was to take up his duties for the night.

He was conscious of the caucophonous noises and was already beginning to differentiate between the different sounds both human and animal. He could distinctly hear the voices of the duty slaves singing in the distance.

He was brought back to his immediate surroundings as he heard Ryder continue, "So our man from England is full of virtue." He instinctively experienced feeling of irritation at the half drunk Ryder, which came out strongly in his reply, "You are a real model person Ryder, are you not?"

"Exactly, Rutherford, you have put your finger on it, I am a model — but for what?"

Wishing to change the interested attempt of the half drunk Ryder and seeking more knowledge of Annie, whom he could not get out of his mind, "Tell me Ryder, how do you reckon Mrs. Palmer? I find it a little disconcerting to find someone so young to be the owner of Rose Hall."

"How do I reckon Mrs. Palmer? You ask me to tell you of the innermost glory and the renowned infamy and temperament of the beauteous lady of great anger and deep sensuality? That I could never do in a few short words." It was almost as if the opportunity to speak of Annie Palmer had breathed new life into Ryder, and even his voice took on a greater air of authority. His obvious poetic attempt surprised Rutherford whose only response was a quiet demand of the facts.

"But really Ryder, you can have as many words as you wish, but give me the facts. As that is where my interest lies."

"Facts, Rutherford, are contemptuous, for they ignore the soul."

"Then tell me Ryder as a start, what happened to John Palmer?"

"John Palmer, sir, did not know the beauty of his bride when he married her at eighteen. He was unable to identify her moods, for indeed when she wanted to please, she would show the greatest innocence. The people in Montego Bay will tell you, sir, that as a little girl, she had left Haiti. Her mother was English and her father an Irish merchant who had come to Haiti on the chance to make money under the reign of King Henry Christophe, who allowed white people to settle there. As a little girl, she somehow became the favourite of a Haitian high voodoo priestess, one of the great influences in King Christophe's court.

"She virtually adopted Annie and showered her with trinkets and gifts. Annie's parents encouraged the interest, as they felt it would enhance their status with the King's court.

"It was the high priestess who had taught Annie to believe in spirits and to realize and recognize that the air was charged with the supernatural, over which she, Annie, could gain control. And so she attended forbidden orgies, summoned up by eerie drum beats in the dead of the night and saw the fear the people had for the high priestess, who schooled her in the ways of invoking fears – black magic and death.

"The priestess convinced Annie that she had the powers of God. When the priestess died, and shortly after Annie's parents' death, in Haiti, instead of returning to England, Annie came to Jamaica, where she met and married John Palmer, in 1820 (as Annie May Patterson) who was himself the Grand Nephew of the late John Palmer whose two sons remained absentee landlords and never visited Jamaica nor Rose Hall nor Palmyra.

"On John Palmer's death, Rose Hall fell to Annie, who then married John McPherson and he himself died leaving Palmyra to Annie. As expected after two husbands, tongues began to wag and the tales spread of her anger and her strength and the power of her trained sorcery, and her beliefs in spirits. This, together with her ability to project death grew, and put real fear in her slaves. As her fame grew, she was the one plantation owner on the Island who was not intimidated by obeah; the slaves would spread the stories of how they believed she spied on them and conjured up fiery tales of doom and death.

"Annie in her solace ruled Rose Hall for several years, while plantation gossip reported a trail of lovers until she married Jameson. "Jameson, it seemed, was after her money. But the slaves reported strange goings on. And when the third husband, the said Jameson was himself found dead, reports of poisoning, stabbing and strangulation grew in strength and there followed an unusual chain of lovers. The public found it hard to reconcile the innocence of the strange deaths of each husband, with the untoward behaviour of Annie.

"Talk of obeah grew and Annie began to run the estate alone, with the assistance of overseers and other white helpers whom she took in as lovers from time to time often also eliciting the help of the overseers to select the choicest of slaves for her satisfaction."

Ryder was fixed on Rutherford, resuming his unsteady posture, and immediately felt he had said too much. Rutherford watched as a mask of fear stretched across his face, and still muttering to himself, he spun around and returned the way he had come.

Rutherford having unpacked was assigned to the still house, his mind a bit clearer, but somewhat overwhelmed by the inferences of Ryder. He felt a need to know more about Annie. His curiosity more than aroused by the ramblings of a drunken Ryder, he tried to separate truth from fiction and began to wonder how much of it he could really believe. How was he to separate truth from fiction?

He arrived and entered the still-house and took charge for the night: almost instinctively moving to the customary high chair, which rested near the wall, and which was usually occupied by all the overseers. He was deep in thought.

As the night time passed, he became increasingly overpowered by the smell of the rum which the slaves were busily engaged in drawing off. This combined with the warm night air and the late hour took its toll on his lack of sleep, and he found that at different times he had to nod himself awake as his head kept falling on to his chest.

This being his first night on the job, he was unaware how keenly the slaves were watching, especially Aaron, who waited to see him doze, and then would dart from behind one vat to another and pull a bottle from its hiding place, and proceed to fill it from the vat and take greedy gulps of the fiery liquid

On this last foray, Aaron, seeing Rutherford sleeping, and boosted by the rum, moved bravely forward, if not steadily, and picked up Rutherford's whip which had fallen to the floor. He proceeded to circle the sleeping Rutherford, and turning to his companions, acted the role of the overseer as he threateningly approached the other slaves in a menacing gesture. They, in turn, were now laughing at the antics of Aaron, which awakened Rutherford.

Rutherford jumped up and quickly looked up to see Aaron with his whip. Almost by remote action, he jumped to the ground and grabbed hold of Aaron by the ear and spun him around. His action drew a gaggle of derision from the other slaves, and a sharp reaction from Aaron, acting in obvious embarrassment.

Rutherford held out his hand for the whip, and as he did this he said, "Now you go dance for the white man."

The other slaves laughed, which angered Aaron further, who threw the whip to the ground at Rutherford's feet. "Pick it up!" Rutherford barked.

But Aaron, with a look of truculence didn't move. Rutherford, with even more venom in his voice, repeated his order. "Pick it up now!" Aaron watched, a savage glare in his eyes, but still made no effort to respond.

Rutherford, his eyes filled with anger, stared at him with full realization of the serious challenge he faced on this his first night – a challenge from which he could not withdraw, and one which he recognized would influence his future ability to perform at Rose Hall. He listened with alarm, his temper rising as he heard the response.

"Pick it up yourself!"

Unable to control himself, and being even more conscious of the response of the other slaves, Rutherford reached out to grab Aaron who with unexpected speed moved away from him, while reaching for the bottle he had hidden earlier. Grabbing hold of the bottle he smashed it against the vat, as he swung around, threateningly, crouching to face Rutherford, who was reaching out to recover the whip which lay between them. Rutherford looked up and braced himself for the obvious attack which he sensed would come. He watched wearily but fully alert as Aaron circled him, but having had to keep his eyes on him, he was unable to reach for the whip; as if in a flash of thought, he decided that offence was the better part of valour and indeed it was going to be his best weapon. Having so decided, he feigned a move to the left, and forced Aaron to lunge and jab at him with the bottle. With almost equal speed he avoided the threat and stepped to the right with a similar feint. Again, Aaron lunged at Rutherford, (with great agility), but as he did so, he expected Rutherford to shift back. Rutherford sidestepped him and landed a crushing right hand blow to Aaron's head which sent him flying. With a somewhat painful right hand, Rutherford watched as he hit the wall and collapsed on the floor.

Just then, on hearing the noise and seeing the skirmish, a couple of overseers came running in. On seeing them Rutherford ordered them in a quiet but seethingly stern voice to take the inert Aaron outside, and revive him, and to send him home when he had recovered.

These instructions, Rutherford could see, had its impact on all as it was not what they were accustomed to, when dealing with unruly slaves.

"Yuh nuh want wi fi lock him up sar?" enquired one of the overseers.

"No. Let him go. He was drunk."

The overseers looked puzzled and a little amazed. "Yuh not going to have him flogged sir?"

"No. Get him out of here. Get back to work the rest of you." Rutherford walked back to his chair. He knew that this kind of reaction by him would both confuse and confound the slaves, but decided that it was the best way to handle the situation. As he moved toward the chair, he saw one of the slaves stoop and pick up the whip which he carried somewhat ceremoniously to hand over to Rutherford, who reached out, and equally ceremoniously took it from his outstretched hand.

Outside the still-house, Aaron stirred and painfully got to his feet. The effect of the rum and the blow had not fully worn off. He was seething with anger and humility, and could only think of revenge. He fumbled down into his trouser leg, pulling out a short sharpened machete and moved toward the door of the still-house.

Peering through the door he saw Rutherford moving from a vat and heading toward the door. He stood back in the shadows, deciding to await Rutherford's exit, knowing that he would also need to breathe some fresh night air, after the encounter.

Rutherford opened the door where he stood silhouetted in the dim light from the fires. Unaware of Aaron's presence, he peered into the darkness and stepped forward to enjoy the cool night air.

But before he could advance more than a step forward, Aaron moved in and tripped him with his feet, sending him sprawling to the ground. Feeling the anger rising within him, Aaron raised the machete and struck at Rutherford, who, on seeing the glint of the machete in the moonlight, skilfully shifted his body away from the blow. Aaron raised his hand to strike again, but as he was about to land the blow, Rutherford saw him look up, and unexplainedly, as if by magic, his face went rigid and his eyes rolled slightly, while he looked vacantly into the night.

The pause allowed Rutherford to jump quickly to his feet, and in one quick movement he swung at Aaron, who was still standing as if in a trance. The blow knocked the machete out of Aaron's hand, and another blow knocked Aaron once again to the ground.

Hearing the rustle and sensing the movement of feet, Rutherford spun around to ward off any further attack. As he glanced in the area of the sound, he saw a tall elderly Negro step forward into the night. He peered into the moonlight and realized that the apparent opposition to Aaron was someone that he vaguely remembered from the auction. "I am Takoo," he said with great authority, and with that, he turned to Aaron, "Let there be no more of this — next time you die, if you do this."

Rutherford watched in some awe, as Aaron nodded dumbly, and with his eyes rolling with fright, scrambled to his feet, and vanished into the night.

Rutherford looked up at Takoo who with a sincere authority in his voice said, "You must watch them all the time, and you must never let them get drunk." His curiosity aroused by this Takoo, Rutherford in turn, and with his now recovered British air, responded, "I'm much obliged, but why did you interfere?"

Takoo in a calm voice, looked at Rutherford and uttered, "I don't like to see murder; do you like to see murder, Mr. White man? And I do not like to see my people hanged, for one day they will be free, and then even Aaron there will learn to walk with pride and dignity." He turned his back on Rutherford and walked off into the night.

Rutherford turned to become aware of the slaves who now gathered at the door of the still house, and being a little exhausted and somewhat disconcerted at the series of incidents, for the first time raised his whip and cracked it in the direction of the slaves, who scattered back into the still-house, without even pausing, as he commanded them, "Get back to work all of you!"

Rutherford moved into the still house and shut the door, as he awaited the final hours of dawn, which was not long in coming. He again felt the heat of the still house as it now contrasted with the morning breeze, which had already begun to ruffle the cane fronds. Before he had closed the door to enter the still house, he could not help but note the great house in the distance, with its stately proportions marked by the shadows of the early morning sun: contrasting with the gang of slaves now moving into the fields, their voices raised in song.

His shift complete, he exited the still-house to watch as Burbridge followed the singing slaves into the fields. As he turned from the door, he looked up to see Ryder approaching him with his long legs almost touching the ground from the back of his mule.

More rested and in a more receptive mood, they exchanged pleasantries, after which he regaled Ryder with the night's activities and recounted the night's tale. Ryder's only comment was, "Unlike you, your horse spent a placid night, and I saw William grooming him this morning."

It was almost as if the incident that took place was as common as the morning sun which now began to light up the estate. Not knowing who William was, and perhaps unprepared for the response of Ryder, he enquired, "Who is William?"

"Which one is William? And why is he tending my horse?"

"William is Mrs. Palmer's stable boy."

"That's very kind of Mrs. Palmer."

"Kind? Why do you say kind my dear fellow? It's not the word I would associate with Annie Palmer — neither her nor Takoo for that matter."

He rode off leaving Rutherford standing in the path surprised and a little bewildered.

Chapter 4

s he watched Ryder ride off into the morning sun, Rutherford, his hand aching from the punches and the exhaustion of the day, slowly crossed the courtyard and walked up the steps and across the verandah. Wearily pushing open the door he crossed the sitting room and entered the welcoming bedroom, which he never thought would have been so accommodating, and indeed pleasant.

He was bone weary and so he flopped heavily on to his bed. This had been an exhausting twenty-four hours for him — certainly a vivid and memorable introduction to Rose Hall.

He bent down to undo his laces, but immediately sensed another presence. He looked up to find Millie standing by his door. She broke into a smile, he could not help but admit through his weariness how charming she looked, immediately realizing that she had taken some care with her appearance. She had her hair neatly bound with a checkered bandana, and her natural beauty and face reflected a most disarming radiance, and her bright black eyes danced with appeal, if just a tinge of mischief.

"You look tired Squire," she said as she stepped over to him and kneeled before him to help unlace his boots.

"If it is not a stupid question," he asked, "Who are you?"

"Me is Millie, Sir." He became even more aware of her presence as he inhaled the appealing pull of her womanly scent. Rutherford stood up, and turned to walk away as he started to unbutton his shirt. Millie, sensing that she had had some effect on him, felt compelled to move and to tease a little. "Don't you like me, Squire?"

With a patient sigh, Rutherford turned, and realizing that he was more moved than he was willing to admit, responded almost impatiently, "When I wake up, I will be willing to discuss your service. Until then, get out of my room!"

Millie pondered briefly at his words, but was not willing to give up that easily, and decided that she would push her advantage further.

"I can cook, sew and read, Squire," she continued. Rutherford, now growing impatient, was not prepared to entertain this anymore. He watched impatiently as she looked at the bed and with a mischievous smile remarked, "You will need to buy a bigger bed, Squire." He watched as she moved her eyes invitingly over his exposed chest and felt her looks create a stirring below his waist, but his stoic British ways held his reserve, and he knew the moment demanded firm action. With that decided, he grabbed Millie firmly by the hand and started to escort her from the room. "However the future works," he said, "sharing my bed will not be a part of it."

Millie pulled back firmly from his grip and continued to smile knowingly. "Where am I going to sleep then, Squire?"

"That I leave to your choice and decision, so good night Ma'am." He pointed to the door and moved threateningly towards her, surprisingly finding that he now found her coquettish smile even more appealing, and wondered if she could sense his feelings.

He could not help but think a little unexpectedly of Annie, and wondered what she might think if she heard of this situation. He was equally unaware of what had preceded this meeting. Responding then with even greater discomfort, he heard Millie remark, "But I am a free girl, you don't have to pay for me if you don't want, Squire."

Rutherford decided to ignore the remarks, especially as he never thought of Millie in terms of money, and with that he stood silently and escorted Millie through the door, realizing how totally tired he was.

Having got rid of Millie, he turned and moved to the bed, which not surprisingly felt as luxurious as any he had ever been in.

Millie was, naturally, pleased with the morning's encounter. It had almost gone as she had wished, and so she continued through the sitting room, where she heard a knock on the front door. She opened it to see William from the great house standing there.

"Massa Rutherford deh here?" asked William of Millie.

"Massa Rutherford asleep."

Not willing to take that as an answer, he pushed past Millie. "A weh yuh a do here?"

"He asleep a tell you," Millie said a little impatiently.

William now totally ignoring her, moved over to Rutherford's door and proceeded to knock politely. Receiving no answer he pushed the door open rather cautiously and peeped into the bedroom. "Massa Rutherford," he called his name gently, and watched as Rutherford struggled slowly upwards with a foul look on his face.

But William knew he had the confidence of the Great House, and so would carry a stronger presence and indeed the support of Annie and Ashman.

"Massa Ashman send mi fi mek you come quick," he said as if to use the name Ashman was good enough to get a response from anyone. "Tell Mr. Ashman I have been up all night, and a bloody savage almost slit my throat, and tell him I can't come now."

"But Massa I bring you horse. It waiting outside and Mr. Ashman seh mi nuh fi leave till you come."

Sensing the authority with which William spoke, and recalling the earlier incidents, too weary to put up a fight, and seeing the determined look on William's face — Rutherford climbed out of the bed and picked up his boots.

As he reached for his boots, he saw Millie re-enter with a small tray and a glass of freshly squeezed orange juice. He saw her slight look of concern, and felt a little compelled to speak, but decided against it.

Rutherford emerged from the half-dark room into the bright sunshine and wearily walked to his saddled horse. With William running ahead, he followed him to his meeting with Ashman. The fresh air of the morning began to make him feel more alert, and rushed his thought on to wishing to get over with the meeting and return to some well-needed sleep. William guided him to a clearing near the boiler house with the still house in the distance, nesting against the backdrop to the ocean. The ride had taken them through some beautiful scenery, but he was too tired to have appreciated all that he saw.

As he drew up to the clearing, he immediately noticed some thirty off duty field men gathered around a man tied to a tree branch. The man was tied high enough, that only his toes touched the ground, and a line of three overseers with their backs to the tied slave faced the field hands.

There was an air of excitement and some agitation among the watchers, as Rutherford rode up. Glancing around to see if he had taken it all in, Rutherford saw Burbridge and Ryder sitting together aboard their mules and a little to the side of the slaves, but they were too far for him to see any response on their faces.

He watched as the overseer moved over to the slave, whom he immediately recognized as Aaron. He saw the overseers move over and violently rip the shirt off Aaron's back. The action almost coincided with the arrival of Annie and Ashman who came galloping into the clearing.

Annie looked unruffled and in full command. As she reined in her horse, a noticeable shiver of apprehension ran through the Negroes. With a look of disdain at this annoying act of a servant, she walked her horse into the clearing.

There was immediate and complete silence, and they all watched as Ashman rode over to Rutherford. "Why did you not report that you were attacked last night?" he asked.

"I punished him myself, and he was drunk." Ashman stared at him and without a blink said, "If he had been sober he would be hanged, not flogged. I am taking into account your inexperience at this job, but in future do not cover up any failure to control labour." Considering the matter final he turned, only to be a little surprised by Rutherford's response.

"I tell you he was drunk, and I dealt with it as I saw fit."

"We are not concerned with what you saw fit. There is only one way to deal with animals like these." Ashman turned to Annie, who nodded her head

Rutherford, recognizing the nod, looked at Annie and was about to appeal to her, when Ashman stopped him cold. "The owner leaves such things to me." Not giving any room for a response, Ashman turned to the overseer, and with a loud voice ordered him to dispense ten lashes on the slave, as he moved over to take his place beside Annie.

Rutherford watched as the overseer slowly raised his whip and delivered the first stroke. The sound of the whip as it buried itself into Aaron's back, elicited a piercing yell from his dry throat, a yell which had a nauseating effect on Rutherford.

He could not help but notice the faces of some of the slaves, with hate burning out of their eyes. On others, he saw a glassy eyed look transcend their features, as they heard the repeated yell of Aaron, and a kind of shudder would pass over them.

Alternatively, another of the overseers raised his whip, and without a changed expression yelled "Two!" as the whip lacerated Aaron's back – "Three!"

" Four!"

The overseer's voice rang out and all but resounded in the clearing, while somewhat balancing, in the mid-morning air, the crack and the yell of Aaron.

Rutherford watched, and could but just see that Ryder had his eyes shut, and that there was a marked strain on his face. He seemed to be muttering to himself. Burbridge on the other hand, showed no emotion. In fact, his countenance differed very little from Ashman's!

"Five!"

Rutherford glanced over at Annie, whose eyes were riveted on the glistening naked body of the slave, her mouth sensuously half open, her tongue caressing her lips, and her flaring nostrils leaving the mark of her breath on the fresh morning mist; he sensed an air of satisfaction and enjoyment emanating from her.

"Six!'

In the short distance to the boiler house, the slaves in the boiler house reacted to the crack of the whip, as they crowded round the barred window some sixty yards away. Their voices echoed a rumble of anger and revolt. The overseer inside, sensing the build-up of anger, jumped among them and cracked his own whip threateningly, deciding that he had best react. Indeed, he had not seen this kind of reaction too frequently.

He watched intently as the cries of Aaron had their effect.

"Seven!"

The rumble from the boiler grew more into a roar and the crack of the boiler house whip now began to have an effect on the Negroes gathered and everyone could now hear the increasing shouts from the boiler house.

"Eight!'

The rumbles increased into intensity and suddenly it seemed as if the slaves were no longer frightened.

"Nine!"

Their faces, Rutherford noticed, were now beginning to turn from fright to rage.

"Ten!"

As the last stroke resounded and Aaron hung unconscious from the tree, Rutherford could see open defiance on the faces of the slaves.

Somewhat wearily, the overseer, his face bathed in sweat, breathing heavily, and with an expression, not dissimilar from that of Annie's reflected on his face, turned to her as they seemed for a moment to share a special sentiment. Rutherford watched as she pulled herself together, and turning to look toward Ashman she nodded. On receiving the nod, Ashman shouted to the overseer to cut Aaron down and send the slaves back to work.

The overseer moved over and began to untie Aaron. Rutherford sensed that the moment was getting out of hand and watched as the slaves refused to move, and the growls and the shouts started up again. He had seen such scenes develop before in the streets of London, as the peasants and the forces of law and order clashed. Somehow, he felt that a revolt was imminent.

The overseers facing the crowd were being pressed backwards and for the first time their whips appeared useless as they lay unpoised to respond. Hate flowed out of the slaves, and they seemed to be thirsty for blood. He felt that they were on the verge of tearing the overseers to pieces. He watched as alarm began to spread across Ashman's face and he instinctively transferred it into action, as he consciously reached for his gun which was strapped to his saddle.

But Annie, ignoring him, spurred her horse forward towards the reacting slaves. Her face was rigid and tense and her eyes burning and withdrawn. Muttering to herself, she continued to approach the slaves. Her approach seemed to further excite the slaves and their voices began to mount with hysteria and excitement as they raised their fists and moved, as if to pull her from the saddle.

Annie was now even closer to the crowd and with her face still tense and her nostrils flaring, the slaves nearest her looked up at her face and recoiled, as did the one next to him and the one next to him, all recoiling like nine pins as she moved her gaze along the line of slaves. Annie never faltered in her pace of forward movement along the line of slaves, and each in turn failed to stand their ground, so that almost as quickly as their anger developed and was quickly replaced by panic.

The mesmerizing effect of the look and presence of Annie had once again placed the advantage with the slave owners. Sensing the developments, Ryder, Burbridge and Rutherford had themselves drawn close to Ashman, who had proceeded to replace his gun as Annie had by now spurred her horse forward, past the slaves who were now running out of the clearing and away from Annie.

Annie wheeled her horse with a smile of triumph playing at the edges of her mouth. She turned and noticed one man at the back who had stood his ground. As she rode towards him, Rutherford looked up and recognized the man as Takoo. As Annie approached him with her smile of triumph, there seemed to be something special between them, some unspoken communication

Ashman rode up to join Annie, and for his part, found Takoo's expression hard to read. But seeking to break the silence said, "I will have them punished for that."

"Let there be no more punishment," Takoo replied.

Ashman was already aware of the spread of discontent which seemed to be increasing and had only now, it appeared, made its way to Rose Hall, and so he felt it incumbent on him to speak strongly to Takoo.

"They killed three overseers over at Myrtle last month," Ashman retorted.

Takoo, his arm folded in defiance, almost disdainfully replied, "The dragoons came and hanged thirty of my people for that, white man! Ten lives for one. Let there be no more whipping; men can be pushed beyond fear to violence."

"Get the labourers back to work, Mr. Ashman," and with a sneering smile at Takoo, Annie wheeled her horse and rode past Burbridge and Ryder, scarcely noticing them, but realizing that they saluted her for her recent actions. On approaching Rutherford, she reined her horse in, noticing that he failed to salute her, "Oh my new and handsome book-keeper disapproves, does he?"

"A book-keeper has no view, Ma'am. He only has bed and board." Noting his dead pan reply, Annie turned, and with her haunting rich laugh, which he remembered from their first meeting, she looked at him with her piercing black eyes, which seemed to almost look through him, "You are learning very quickly, Mr. Rutherford. Such aptitude must be encouraged, don't you think?"

And turning to Ashman, "Mr. Ashman would you see that our new bookkeeper is cleared of duties this evening." Rutherford could not help but notice the anger in Ashman's eyes as Annie departing said to him — "We dine at nine."

Ashman approached her saying, "I don't think this possible, Mrs. Palmer."

"You heard me, Mr. Ashman," was Annie's curt reply.

"But Mrs. Palmer, we are to visit Palmyra this evening and we can scarcely complete the inspection by this evening."

"Represent me Mr. Ashman, you do it so ably. I have every confidence in you." She turned back to Rutherford and said "At nine then Mr. Rutherford. Dress as you would at home." And with a smile, she turned her horse and galloped full tilt towards the Great House, leaving Rutherford with mixed emotions, tiredness and anticipation.

Rutherford, his weariness once again erupting over him, turned and nodded at Ryder and Burbridge, as he spurred his horse to head back to his house. Deep in thought, but weary at this most exhausting day, he immediately headed to his room, where in seconds he was fast asleep.

Chapter 5

Millie continued to be busy around the house and in the yard, her mind continually occupied by the thoughts about the man she referred to as Squire, but always being ever mindful of Takoo's advice to her.

On the other hand, Psyche, recoiling with fear at the earlier incident, kept her distance and busied herself with Burbridge's chores.

Millie poured the bucket of hot water, which she had heated up for her master, into a large tin tub; she carefully tested the water with her finger, and with a knowing smile, rearranged the towels and the brush and soap.

The tin tub occupied a secret and unobtrusive side of the verandah which was curtained off by burlap and represented the best that Rose Hall could offer to its Junior Staff of book keepers.

Millie rose and surveyed the room to ensure that everything was to her liking. Satisfied, she left, and crossed the empty living room, where an oil lamp was now burning for her master, the Squire, a name he disliked. He had slept the rest of the day away, but it was now time to awaken him.

She picked up a glass of orange juice from the kitchen and walked without knocking, into the master's room; she entered leaving the door ajar, so as to allow what light there was to come in from the living room, for night fell quickly and sharply at Rose Hall. She moved to sit at the foot of his bed, and looked at Rutherford affectionately, while engendering enough courage to wake him. She shook him firmly, but gently by his foot. "Squire yuh bath ready."

Rutherford stirred weakly and wiped his eyes, recognizing Millie. "Oh, it's you?!"

She handed him the juice and he quickly drank it. "What time is it, Millie?"

"Time to get up Squire. The Missus, our white witch, will vex if you keep her waiting." The reminder from Millie brought back hurriedly to his mind the happening of the day and his immediate meeting that lay ahead.

He rose to notice that the clothes he had removed were missing, and in its place was freshly starched and ironed clothes, which were all neatly laid out; with his cuff links and personal items neatly stacked beside them with even the feminine touch of flowers now residing in a tumbler on the so called dresser.

Impressed, he remarked to Millie his appreciation, but added, "but let's come to a clear understanding. I won't come to your bedroom, and you will stay out of mine."

Millie, ignoring his comment, merely enquired, "Are you always in a bad mood when yuh wake up, master?" and then added, "I haven't got a bedroom."

Becoming more annoyed, Rutherford retorted, "My room is private. Do not come in unless you knock. If you are not aware, then learn, for it is the quality of our privacy which separates us from animals." His voice rose in authority as he spoke, and he left no doubt as to his feelings and the import of his words.

But Millie did not seem to make any of this mean anything to her as she handed him his robe and slippers. "First time I see you master I know yuh was no ordinary book-keeper."

Millie still calmly ignoring Rutherford's commands to privacy, took him to the tub, where Rutherford ordered her not to enter, despite her teasing entreaty to scrub his back.

Speaking to Millie from the tub, as she waited patiently outside the sacking Rutherford said, "I think I heard you call my employer a 'white witch' and I don't think she would treat that as a compliment, so from now on keep a respectful tongue."

"But Squire is not because I jealous I call her dat, but is because lot a people die up dere, and they die funny, and I see you mind already wid her. But tek care Squire – a lot of people die up there."

Rutherford completed his bath, singing to himself, in serious anticipation of his visit, almost completely ignoring Millie's protestations as mere gossip, superstition and envy. He returned to his room and carefully completed his dressing, donning the latest London fashion which he had treated himself to before leaving home.

Mounting his horse, he enjoyed the fresh sea breeze which usually made this time of night cool and invigorating; and with the compliment of soft moonlight and a bright starlit sky, he felt a tremor of anxiety as he anticipated even more so, the upcoming evening's repast with the beautiful Annie. But then, even as he did so, he found a tinge of caution pulling at the edges of his mind.

Revisiting the site of his first arrival, although now at night, he could still vividly recall the beauty of the outside view. As he reached the park and pulled the bell cord, it was to have the doors almost immediately thrown open by William if in eager anticipation of his arrival.

Rutherford was even more impressed by the interior view as the open mahogany door revealed a magnificent carved mahogany staircase which led to the upper floors. Occupying pride of place and balancing the magnificent staircase and hall was the finest chandelier, and a Venetian candelabra which hung from the high ceiling, offering a soft glow to the hall.

He had very little time to see much more of this beautiful setting as his eyes were drawn to the top of the staircase where Annie stood formally dressed, in contrast to the riding habit he had only seen her in before.

Her dress cut in a low *delcotte* with a wide crinoline of enchanting hue wrapped her in an air of fragile sophistication. Rutherford stepping forward could only say "A radiant and most beautiful sight Ma'am – one fit only for a king and not a jaded book-keeper." Annie with a smile descended and in that rich voice of hers: "Good evening Mr. Rutherford", and with that she moved sensuously towards him, allowing him to take her hand and bow.

Annie turned to William and nodded as he opened the double doors leading to the drawing room. The drawing room overwhelmed Rutherford even more than the entrance hall. Its some six hundred square feet of space engulfed them both into the belly of its opulence and ornate beauty, and reminded Rutherford of the great ducal houses of England — its only contrast with England was the warmth of the Caribbean night and the presence of a barefooted house slave standing like a Presidium Guard overlooking the sideboard which itself was tastefully complimented by the wide choice of the best liquors.

"Sherry? Whisky? What will it be Mr. Rutherford? I take it you have already had your fill of rum."

"Sherry if you please."

Turning to the servant Annie ordered two sherries, having decided to join her guest in his choice of drinks.

She beckoned Rutherford to sit in the deep armchair which faced her as she moved over to sit on the sofa which was set at a right angle to the elaborately carved fireplace, over which hung a large and striking portrait of Annie.

"Permit me Ma'am but I was told to expect to see wealth in the West Indies but very little was ever said of beauty and taste."

"So we are thought of as barbarians in England, are we?"

As the servant served the drinks, Rutherford turned, pondering the scene and becoming more relaxed to Annie and raising his glass "Ignorance I fear Ma'am. To Rose Hall, its elegance and its enchanting loveliness." Annie smiled and looked at Rutherford and revelled in the moment.

"You are smooth with your words Mr. Rutherford, but you must not judge a woman by her pomander or the cut of her crinoline. If I may ask Mr. Rutherford, why have you come to Jamaica?"

It was as direct a question as Rutherford expected but gaining his composure, he thoughtfully reflected, "My father, Ma'am."

"Would you use my name Annie? I find the use of Ma'am rather trite!"

"I dared not make that presumption, Ma'am."

"I would so presume if I were you," said Annie, "but tell me, really, why are you here in Jamaica?"

A little rattled, Rutherford became somewhat cross at the continued questions by Annie and others, and replied a little sharply, "Why does everyone want to find this out? But for the record, my father owns a plantation in Barbados. What then is more natural..." With the flash of her hand Annie leaned forward and cut him short, taking his hand, she looked directly at him with her wide black eyes and spoke almost mysteriously, "I think you killed a man Robert. I see trees, an early morning mist, a dark tall man and a woman in red weeping; the man's name is Crawford – no Corriman!"

Rutherford could now no longer retain himself and very visibly shaken, almost involuntarily said, "Sherman! Mrs. Palmer, I, thought nobody knew."

Annie with a satisfied smile on her face leaned back on the sofa enjoying the look of utter surprise on Robert's face. "I will take another sherry Robert, and fill up your glass also, will you?"

Rutherford went to the sideboard and returned with the two glasses of sherry.

"Did you love her very much?"

"Yes. Damn it, I did! How did you know?"

"They call me the white witch of Rose Hall, don't you know? I am sure you know that witches do strange things, such as seeing into minds and thoughts."

"I usually dismiss such things as idle gossip and fantasies of the mind."

"Oh! Poor Robert. Grown men can be so gullible; but sleep assured that I am no witch, but I have known witches while in Haiti. You see, my parents were killed there when the slaves revolted, and I was shipped off to the English Island by a friend. So while you were attending genteel English schools I romped in the forests of Haiti, with the children of the voodoo priests and learned about Maitresse and Erzoulee and other forest gods."

Learning this, Rutherford thought how true Ryder's account was and a look of concern tinged with pity crossed his face.

"You needn't pity me Robert! I was happy there and the training robbed me of my inhibitions and prepared me for the life of this plantation and certainly taught me how to use my smattering of voodoo to replace the excessive use of the whip on the slaves. That's why there has never been a slave revolt on Rose Hall."

"But certainly this has created problems with your neighbours and other planters."

"That, Robert, does not concern me as I don't encourage them to visit. They call me what they want. My slaves call me a white witch, but I own and run the most successful, biggest and best plantation on the island of Jamaica."

As Annie completed her retort, they were interrupted by Leila the maid, who entered to announce (in impeccable French) that dinner was ready.

Rising, Annie offered her arm and escorted Rutherford into the dining room.

At the centre of the long mahogany table, built to hold some seven times their number stood two bare-footed servants facing each other behind two chairs before which were set the tools for dining. Rutherford as expected, saw that this room also was in keeping with what he had seen so far.

As they moved to sit, he leaned over, and in whispering tones said.

"Would that person, I mean Leila, be the friend from Haiti?"

"You are improving Robert, and becoming quite insightful"

"That business about the duel? Even the man's name, I am sure was a lucky shot — a shot in the dark. A case of a shrewd estimation of an English gentleman."

Smiling at him, her eyes shrouded for a moment, and she muttered, "How perceptive". She smiled knowingly as she invited Robert to feast.

Chapter 6

Following Rutherford's departure, Millie made her way down the footpath to the slave huts some not unlike the book-keepers quarters she had just left.

Sitting in the clearing were some women and a few children tending the fires which were meant to smoke away the mosquitoes rather than to provide warmth.

Millie spoke to one of the women, who moved and entered the nearest hut. Inside the room, Takoo was sitting on a wooden stool, bedecked in his bracelets and a feathered head dress; he was speaking to some fifteen slaves who were squatting in a conclave around him, listening intently.

"Spread the word that the white man's King has finally been shamed into passing a law to set us the Negroes free in all the kingdoms he owns. But the Governor only talks of it and is afraid if he enforces it, the planters will rebel and not obey."

"What good is the law then if the white man will not obey?" asked one of the conclave members.

Takoo pointed out, "Even if the planters do not obey, the dragoons will, and this will give us the Spirit to fight for our rights ourselves."

The woman who had entered used the pause and called to Takoo.

"What is it woman?" The woman at his voice knelt and bowed her head and stopped at a respectful distance.

"What is it woman?"

"Your grand-daughter is waiting Nona." She bowed and disappeared out of the room.

Takoo, without much reaction, continued his instructions, "We will not kill for the sake of killing. When the time comes we will rise as one – from Myrtle to Fair Isle, from Ironshore to Valley Pen, from St. Catherine to Morant Bay — we will take Jamaica and build a new Negro Nation like Christophe of Haiti who has promised us his support with arms and soldiers. Go back now to your people quickly, before you are missed. Peace be with you and may the gods protect you as the spirit of our ancestors rise before us." He gave the sign of dismissal, rose and left the room.

He crossed the clearing to his abode and entered to find Millie, sitting on a stool.

The room was bare except for an oil lamp on the floor and a scattering of stools and a collection of pots, calabashes and African carvings

Millie rose and bowed to Takoo. "Tell me," he said smiling, "how does your new white husband treat you?"

"He is a good man," replied Millie.

"Good! When the day comes we will need men like him; very few of our people see beyond the day of freedom to drink and laze in the sun, and play with women. And you, how do you feel?"

"I could learn to love him," replied Millie haltingly, scornfully adding "but she has sent for him already. Please, Takoo, please, give me obeah that will protect him."

Takoo looked closely at her, as a small tear edged from her eyes and her face showed sadness, as she continued, "Make me stronger than she. Nona, make me strong like you. Let me learn from you so that I can protect him."

Chapter 7

Rutherford and Annie, having finished dinner, toyed with each other in thought over their coffee cups. Their glasses of brandy stood expectantly before them, and the flickering candlelight revealed faces that were flushed with wine. A soft breeze blowing from the sea rustled the curtains as Annie spoke.

"Do I believe in spirits? What a question Robert. Do you believe in air? In water? In death? In love? In hate? In fear? And all of these revelations of the soul? Oh I know one never usually talks of this over coffee... But I have learned to accept such things as real."

Rutherford looked at her reflectively and found he was responding with surprising candidness. "I don't believe I ever thought of death. I have of course in my life come close to it and have heard of the spiritual world; but now you plunge me into the world of witchcraft, obeah and such evils."

"Robert why do you use the words expounded by missionaries, who equally dismiss Eastern faiths as pagan? How can I make you see? When you were in love, did she not have power over you? And when it ended, you grieved, and if she had died would you not have grieved more? Was the bond not there, and would she not have lived with you in spirit? Now translate that to the plane of ecstasy and into the romantic plane. I can see as I speak of romance and mysticism, I see you are uncomfortable.

"Suppose the spirit world does exist, and some people do reach it, imperfectly at times, I do agree, and by so doing they use that same kind of ritual, which I may add is able to contain the violence usually attributed to such experiences."

"But are you not frightened by it? And living here alone in a house where so many have died?" Rutherford seemed to be continually carried away by the conversation as Annie continued as if there had not been a response.

"The familiar holds no terror for me Robert, and the stories have led the slaves to believe that the ghosts of those who died here, haunt both inside and outside; they say they see shapes that move and they hear voices — so nothing comes near here at night; believe me Robert I sleep very well at night."

Finishing her response and feeling the continued warmth of the wine, Annie rose almost abruptly, as if disturbed.

"Would you like to see the rest of the house Robert?"

Rutherford himself buoyed by the strength of the wine, turned to Annie and asked, "Did you kill them Annie?"

Almost flippantly but with a desolate look, she smiled, "Is it considered good manners in Bristol to accuse your hostess of murder and would it matter if I had?"

"Tonight Annie, nothing would matter to me except the candlelight in your eyes and the urge I feel to remove the loneliness I see in your eyes."

"Listen Robert Rutherford, since we are now friends and lies are of no use in a friendship, I speak of this once more only, and I forbid either one of us to ever speak of it again. John Palmer died of ague. He was a weak man, but I am grateful to him, for he was one man who loved me for myself. He was a kind and gentle man, who gave me the only home I ever knew, and I grieved for him. As for the others they married me only for Rose Hall; and as God would have it they all died of a fever and never grieved for them. On the contrary I was glad and relieved."

"Glad?" Rutherford asked

"Why are you surprised Robert?" she paused took a breath and asked, "How did you feel?"

"I killed a man Annie, and I felt no guilt." As they walked and talked Rutherford could feel a bond of closeness developing and as he looked at Annie leading him up the staircase, he was even more mesmerized by her beauty which was reflected under the flickering lights of the candelabra she held in her hand.

"Robert I have loved this house ever since I first saw it, but it is much too big for my use alone. And as you can see most of the rooms are unused, and are merely dusted and maintained, as I do very little outside entertaining."

She opened the door to what was obviously her room and Rutherford's eyes were immediately drawn to the elegant canopied four poster bed; and next to the door leading to the sitting room was the most exquisite Queen Anne slant desk with a heavy rug between the door and the bed. Annie placed the candelabra on the desk and opened the windows which looked out into the dark night, where the fireflies created their flickering pattern against the sea beyond.

Rutherford moved over to where Annie stood gazing into the night as a soft puff of wind blew out one or two of the candles.

"Whether it be night or day," Annie remarked, "the view is magnificent."

Rutherford almost compulsively reached for her hand as he pulled her closer to him and turned her around to place his lips fiercely on hers, and almost as if realizing the fierceness of the embrace they both pulled away simultaneously, almost as if surprised by the violence of the embrace, and yet unable to withstand the compelling force.

"Unhook me Robert." Annie turned her back on him.

With anxious passionate fingers, Rutherford unhooked Annie's blouse and pulled down her crinoline, and as she moved to aid him in his — at times — masculine ineffectiveness, she disrobed him also.

As they moved to the welcoming bed and the comforting arm of each other, Rutherford reached over and kissed her gently, and proceeded to remove her chemise. They both grasped each other in passionate embrace.

Rutherford entered her with almost uncontrolled passion and felt her fingers bite into his shoulder blade as she mouthed unrecognisable words and urged him to an exploding frenzy of passion.

Lying abated in their passion, Annie was aroused from her reverie almost simultaneously with Robert, by the ringing of the bell and the response of Leila, *"J'arrive, J'arrive"*, and they heard the withdrawal of the bolts.

Annie rose in obvious anger and reached for her dressing gown as she moved purposefully out of the room. As she saw Ashman, she moved to push Leila out of the way and coldly barked at him.

"Don't treat my servants like your field hands, Mr. Ashman." Her voice was cold and piercing. "And now Mr. Ashman, what is it that could not wait till the morning?" Rather flustered but seeking to control his obvious raging temper, Ashman proceeded to advise Annie of a slave meeting he had witnessed at Palmyra and how he felt it could lead to bigger things. He advised how he felt that it would need investigating and as he would have to be away he would need the new man to visit the docks to see to the docking of the Santa Rosa and the loading of the Rum.

Rutherford had by this moved to the desk to listen to the exchange and heard Annie say, "Why could not that wait till in the morning?"

"Because the wagons leave at six," Ashman replied rather cynically, "and I wondered if you would tell Rutherford or if you wanted me to do it.

Rutherford saw Annie's face turn white with anger as she started to re-ascend the stairs, but turning, round calmly slowly spoke.

"I'll tell him, and, for the record John, both your manners and your temper need addressing, and it may be wise if you remember that good managers are not all that hard to find." He gave her a hard look but said no words.

Rutherford could feel the steely tension as Ashman muttering, turned and stormed out of the room as Leila closed the door on his exit.

Annie smiled at Robert as she re-entered the room, and guided him gently back to the bed, and it was as if the incident had stirred even deeper emotions in them both. They virtually clawed at each other in wild abandonment. The only interruption came when the mosquito net came hurtling down locked in the passion of a heavy climax.

Chapter 8

Rutherford rose at the crack of dawn and gazed at Annie, who seemed lost in childlike slumber, but stirred and whispered what sounded like Darling book-keeper. His mind turned with some hate on Ashman, but recalling what Annie had told him of the incident, he dressed quietly and headed for the door.

As he arrived, he noticed Burbridge on the verandah in his freshly washed clothes, and close by several ox-drawn carts loaded with barrels, which he presumed were the ones he would have to accompany to the docks and which Ashman used as the reason for his visit to Rose Hall. At the thought of it, he smiled playfully.

The morning air had a slight chill to it and the overseer who was with the workers watched closely as the slaves stood around slapping themselves to keep warm.

Rutherford felt very conspicuous and self-conscious as he rode into the courtyard, especially as he was still dressed in his evening clothes. Embarrassed, he hurriedly rushed past the obviously intrigued Burbridge and charged into his room. As he entered, he immediately noticed that his work clothes were neatly laid out washed and ironed. He dressed quickly. He looked up to see Millie patiently standing by the door, holding in her hand a travelling bag which she handed to him as he headed for the verandah.

He did not have time to notice the look of disapproval on her face as she moved to pick up the clothing he had discarded from his evening's outing, which she piled neatly in the corner of the room. She hustled out of the door heading in the same direction as Rutherford.

Millie arrived just as the leading wagon was heading out the drive, and with that done, she climbed on her mule, and spurred him to ride side by side with Rutherford and to catch up with the wagons which were moving out at a fair clip through the countryside, at times losing itself in the cloud of dust which shimmered in the early morning sunrise as the carts and the oxen and mules disturbed the inert dust.

In the distance, Rutherford thought he saw two riders who looked like Annie and Ashman, but could not be clear and decided to dismiss it from his mind, especially after reflecting on the night before.

It seemed the wagons were now moving slower as the day turned into mid-morning and Rutherford found himself nodding from the exhausting activity of the night. Millie continued to stay close to him, when suddenly she turned her mule and galloped over to the overseer whom she had known very well before and whispered to him, after which she rode back to Rutherford and halted his horse, turning him down a side path. The intrusion awakened Rutherford and he opened his eyes to see the wagons moving away from him. Before he could speak, Millie advised him that she would be taking him through a short cut.

"It is a short cut Squire, and it will take four more hours before we are down the hill and this will give us a head start and allow you to get some rest."

Worried about the safety of the rum and still not knowing who to trust, Rutherford began to protest.

"Squire, the overseer and the men are from my tribe and I have spoken to them. The rum is safe, safer than if you were there."

Being too tired to protest, he listened as Millie went on, "We could have lunch and you can rest Squire and I promise No Trick."

Rutherford considered the offer and found it tempting, but started to rein his horse back towards the wagons.

"Squire you have a piece of paper and a pencil?" His curiosity aroused, he asked why.

"Squire please write for me: 'If anything happens to the wagons or the rum, I Millicent, grand daughter of Takoo, agree to be sold as a slave.' Now let me sign." Rutherford noticed the impish smile on her face as she knowingly won the point and led him down the hill, away from the wagon.

After a short distance, he could hear the sound of water and saw Millie stop in the distance. As he rode up, he saw Millie dismount from her mule and reach for a bag on her saddle, from which she began to unpack under the shade of a large banyan tree. In this obviously romantic setting, Millie laid out the makings of lunch and reached behind Rutherford's saddle for the bag she had earlier given him, from which she unpacked soap and sharing utensils.

"Tell me Millie, is this the way you're efficient at all times? And is this how you serve all your masters?"

"Not really, Squire. You see, I like you and you would be a good father for my children."

"But if you adopt this for all your masters, you will have quite a family. Have you had many jobs before this?"

Rutherford was not a little surprised at the fierceness in her voice as she replied, "No man ever touch me yet Squire," and as he turned to look in her direction he saw her quietly slipping out of her dress. He was surprised to find himself responding to the slow and graceful movements she made as she walked towards the spray and spume of the waterfall. It seemed as if she was laughing and taunting him with the sway of her hips and the lithesomeness of her step, as she entered the water and moved upward and the water caressed her shapely thighs.

"You think I am jealous because you sleep with another woman; the women of my tribe are accustomed to our men having many wives. Annie Palmer don't hurt me Squire—you will come back to me when you ready and finish with her, cause I look after you and I care for you and you know I better than she! I 'fraid fi what she will do to you, for if anything happen to you mi heart would break."

Rutherford stopped sharing and looked in her direction.

"You are a strange girl Millie, and it seems that everyone here believes in duppies and ghosts. As for me Millie I can only take a woman to bed when I respect her. Perhaps I am a victim of my British upbringing."

He turned to continue sharing and failed to see as Millie came out of the pool and gracefully moved towards him. As she came up to him, she took the towel he had draped around his neck and pulled him towards her body, at the same time placing his hand on her breasts.

He could all but resist the cool touch of her body as it glowed in the filtering dim light through the branches of the trees. He felt himself respond as she pulled him gently to the ground and reached to unbuckle the belt of his pants.

"Come my Squire. Come and share the love Millie has for you." Rutherford felt the cool of her body change to warmth and took the taut extent of her full dark youthful breast in his mouth. It tasted fresh from the river water.

As they lay on the ground rolling around in the dim light of the tree, he could smell the strength of the earth in his nostrils and it seemed to imbue him with more vigour as he responded to the wild and abandoned movements of Millie.

He had never felt so free while making love, and wondered later if it was because he was doing the act with only the earth, the sky and the trees as his companions.

The wagons were parked at the side of the road as Rutherford and Millie emerged from the side road, and Rutherford realized they had been waiting for some time, but he was too embarrassed to say anything, and relieved to see the wagons he rode slowly past each wagon, inspecting the casks to see if they had been tampered with.

Millie watched him carry out the inspection with silent amusement and enquired of the overseer if they had been waiting long.

"'Bout two hours, Massa," came the reply. He looked at Millie, slightly embarrassed, but she merely carried an impish grin on her face.

A troop of white Cavalry passed, and Rutherford used the moment to tear up the paper on which he had written Millie's pledge. As he glanced up, he saw the port in the distance and the sailing vessel lying in wait to receive the Rose Hall cargo.

Their arrival at the port took Rutherford's mind off the thoughts he was sharing with himself, as the dock men began the unloading of the barrels from the carts to the ship.

He assisted with the unloading until the empty wagons were taken away and they all headed for the tavern where Millie had seen to his horse. He procured drinks for the now exhausted slaves who gathered round and drank the mugs of coffee served to them.

One by one, they flopped on the straw where they would spend the night before returning to Rose Hall.

Rutherford made his way inside the tavern to the room they had prepared for him. He was tired, exhausted and a little troubled, his mind wondering as to where Annie and Ashman were heading when he saw them in the distance.

He wondered if he was a little jealous, and seemed almost unaware of Millie's presence and the recent time he spent with her—Annie was at the forefront of his mind and the forebodings were not comforting to his evening's rest.

As he glanced through the window and noticed the dark clouds drawing close, he heard the loud clap of thunder it somehow seeming to sound an alarm.

Chapter 9

"*mericus, Dorky, Caesar*", Annie called out as she hunched over the estate books spread out before herself and Ashman. "You remember some two years ago, were those not runaways, was that not the time we found them at Stony Gut? And tell me, have there been any more pregnancies at Palmyra?" The mention of Stony Gut immediately conjured up one word—Rebellion.

"Yes, two grass cutters," replied Ashman. "We'll take care of it."

Having completed the work, Annie turned to him and teasingly said, "John, your pretty girl Clorinda, how is she? And by the way, how is the loading in Montego Bay?"

"Well enough by all accounts."

"When will they be back, today or tomorrow?"

Realizing that her thoughts were back on Rutherford, Ashman, somewhat addled, spoke on, "Annie I am no good at this, but I have spent these past three years with you and seen Rose Hall prosper. From the day we first became lovers, I have wanted you. It's not like you to let yourself be fooled by this chap from Bristol. And one who has already taken a slave for his bed."

He watched the look that crossed Annie's face. He knew it would hurt, "and even more, she is the grand-daughter of Takoo — quite a beauty."

"No, you lie!" cried Annie, and with that she stalked out angrily and rushed up to her room. Racing over to her dressing table, and still aware of the smell of Rutherford, she grabbed the mirror and staring at the mirror she pulled at the small lines that lay faintly around her eyes. Sensing the quiet presence of Leila who had entered the room, she turned to her and said, "Look! I am getting old."

"*Non Ma Jolie, toi pas vieue de tout,*" she soothed Annie as she sobbed in the arms of her beloved Leila, who seemed to know her every need.

As was customary after the loading of the ship, the Rose Hall wagons, as those of all other Estates did, would gather in the courtyard of the tavern before returning to the Estate, which would be in the late evening following the previous day. By this time, the onerous chores having been completed, it was time for revelry, and the drinking would continue from the early morning hours, right into the evening of departure.

Rutherford watched as the local Mento band, dressed in a motley of colours, arrived to add spice and revelry to the occasion, with a banjo, violin and some by the rhumba box. The music started as the local Montego Bay merchants arrived with a number of the local courtesans. It would not be long before Rutherford would witness the limbo competition which would start soon.

With the sound of the limbo tune, Rutherford watched as with all eyes riveted on Millie. She approached the horizontal bar. On her arrival, it was lowered to some nine inches from the ground. With a great deal of amusement on her face, and seeing Rutherford, Millie sensuously approached the bar arched her back and invitingly swayed her hips moving under the bar with consummate ease. Flushed, she rose laughing and moved gracefully to Rutherford, and with a nervous smile invited him to join her. "I will break in two, and what good would I be then?" was his only retort. Moving even more provocatively, Millie turned to the onlookers who were urging her to take

Rutherford into the dance. Sensing that one or two spectators were beginning to believe he was afraid, and at the urging of Millie, Rutherford moved to the centre of the ring of dancers and found that he was caught up in the hypnotic sound of the music, followed Millie towards the pole, which the girls now raised to a higher level. Despite Millie's help, Rutherford was only able to make it half way under the bar when he collapsed unceremoniously to the ground, amidst the cheers and jeers of the onlookers.

Millie felt a little embarrassed, and taking his hand led him back from the pole, she laughingly bent over to Rutherford and whispered something to him. As the music continued, she led him forward once again, and this time he glided under the bar to the shouts of the crowd.

Rutherford smiled triumphantly as Millie said, "You see? And now seeing that I am Queen, you are King!" She crowned him with a plait of straw which she had quickly woven from a bale in the nearest wagon.

Fully charged with his achievement, Rutherford headed for the bar. As he moved up, he noticed the presence of Bannion, one of the estate's lawyers, next to him. "Well, well, you are now quite one of us, aren't you?"

"I do my best," Rutherford replied as he turned to Millie, who looked rather crossly at Bannion.

The feelings between them was becoming visible, as Millie whispered something in Rutherford's ear and flounced off with a disdainful look at Bannion.

"Would it be improper for me to enquire where you met her? You are a lucky man Rutherford — not ten days on the plantation and you have the most sought after mulatto virgin in Jamaica."

Rutherford chose to ignore Bannion's question as he departed the bar to catch up with Millie who had gone to the fields and was now joining him to head to the inn, and the promise of staying close to her new found master.

As they wandered away from the crowd, Rutherford could feel the envy of all eyes, and sensing this Millie drew closer to Rutherford as they headed for his room.

Rutherford felt the passion building up inside him. As Millie entered the room behind him, she remarked at her dislike for the drinking of the men. "Squire even when I wear clothes they make me feel naked — they only want my body."

"And what makes you think I am any different?" he replied.

The remark registered on Millie almost immediately and as it sank in, she jumped up at Rutherford and they both fell unto the bed. Furiously ripping at her clothes and overcome with desire, Rutherford possessed Millie's body with unknown passion as they both enjoyed the feel and earthy smell of each other.

As the morning dawned, Rutherford could hear the sounds of the workers preparing to depart. He glanced at Millie, who had begun to stir from the deep sleep of satisfaction.

Dressing quietly and a little embarrassingly, Millie turned to Rutherford and asked, "Squire will you tell her?"

Rutherford pondered the question and replied, "If she asks me."

"Do you know she can send me away from Rose Hall? Squire don't let's go back to Rose Hall. I am afraid. Squire if I ask you to do something for me, would you do it? Something really big?"

"I doubt it."

"But Squire I want you to come with me to see my grandfather."

The request, was not in keeping with Rutherford's expectations, but he found no difficulty in telling Millie that he would be delighted to make the acquaintance of the other gentleman.

"Just a social visit — is it Millie?"

"Well Master, when one is going to take a bride, is it not the custom to ask the blessings of the girl's family?"

Startled at this quite alarming response Rutherford sat up suddenly and realized he had to put a stop to this. "I like you Millie, but somehow I don't see myself visiting your grandfather for this reason".

"You are afraid, like all white men, of marriage, but Squire in our tribe when a man has taken a woman, even for a day, she is his woman, and if I don't take you to my grandfather, he will consider me a loose woman." Recalling the pleasurable passion they had both shared and feeling the strong pull of Millie and sensing how much it would mean to her, he found himself responding humorously.

"No tricks?"

"No master, no tricks, but would you want me to sign another paper?" Rutherford looked at her mischievous smile and could only raise his hands as he contemplated the eventuality.

"I suppose as always you are well ahead of me, and I would not be surprised if you told me that we are not too far from your grandfather's house." Smilingly, Millie reigned her horse and headed northerly, knowing that Rutherford would be following right behind her.

They arrived at Takoo's village amidst the din of domestic activities. In the centre of the village, one could see the women cooking, chicken and goats roaming in between the houses.

Takoo greeted them with his calabash in his hand, having just come from sprinkling its contents on the floor before the shrine where he had just prayed in Iwi and Fanta for the guidance of the god over the lives of the young people of the village.

Takoo beckoned them into his house, and as he entered, he remarked, "It is good in these very restless times, that all our people should come together and ... " pausing as if he recognized the uncontrollable movement towards the inevitable, he turned to Rutherford and intently said, " — look after her."

Robert remarked, "I am already beholden to you, and this will make it more than once."

Holding up his hand to silence Rutherford, he turned to Millie, "You will obey him in all things, as you would me," and, earning her agreed response, he said to Rutherford, "She is my favourite, and I have spoiled her. Be strong and strict with her, and don't be afraid to chastise her from time to time. It will do her a world of good; and I am glad you both have shown to this man the honour of coming to see him."

Takoo rose from his stool, as Millie rose and gave a curtsy to depart.

Exiting into the sunlight, Rutherford blinked and mounted his horse and they rode out of the bare dirt compound and down the footpath towards the cane fields.

Reflecting on the words of Takoo, he remarked to Millie, "It is a great pity that our Annie Palmer does not see the impending problems and use the breadth of approach like your Takoo to improve the situation.

And kneeing his horse, he headed off at a speed to catch up with the wagons.

As they approached Rose Hall and the wagons headed for the stables, Rutherford waved them goodbye, and looked up at the house where he sensed the eyes of Annie Palmer had been looking at them.

They arrived at the residence, and Psyche greeted them and accompanied Millie and the Squire's trunk into the bedroom. She watched intently as Millie began to unpack, and with a satisfied smile on her face, took out one of her dresses which she hung up next to Rutherford's clothes while Psyche looked on wide-eyed and knowing.

Millie turned around and embraced Psyche as they both hugged and spun round laughing.

Hearing Rutherford's footsteps approach, they broke off, as Rutherford entered and greeted Psyche.

"Welcome back Massa," she replied as she scuttled from the room.

Millie continued her unpacking, anxiously waiting to see if he had noticed her new domestic decisions. Realizing that he had not, she decided to take the bull by the horns.

"Squire, we forgot to buy something in Montego Bay?"

"And what was that may I ask?"

"A big bed for the two of wi", and with that she rushed over to hug Rutherford, who responded with a hug of his own.

Millie, however, could not shake the eerie feeling which came over her. She found herself whispering, "Oh Master take care, please take care..."

Chapter 10

The overnight rain had softened the baked and parched earth and, as was customary, the air responded with a rich earthy smell silently applauded by the waving refreshed leaves which danced and swayed in the evening light.

The solitude of the evening did nothing to Annie's mood. As she moved away from the curtained window to the dining table, she asked Leila to serve her coffee while she waited. By the time the coffee arrived, she was seething with rage. Leila set the cup down and walked away, she swept the coffee cup off the table and it landed with a crash, which caused Leila to spin around and come speeding back with a rush, only to be pushed aside by Annie as she stormed from the table.

Intent on what she saw earlier, her blood continued to boil. She made up her mind, and ordered her horse to be saddled, and without bothering to look right or left or even to consider her attire, she headed for the book-keepers' quarters.

Annie arrived at the quarters a little before Rutherford returned home from his shift at the still-house. Just as she entered the parlour/hall, she could hear his footsteps ascending the stairs to the verandah which ran the full length of the house.

As he entered the hall, he saw the fury building up on her face and wondered what he could do to prevent what seemed to be the inevitable.

"I have been expecting you to come and see me," she said, hoping against hope.

Rutherford responded evenly, "Annie! I have had a very hard day."

"So this is where you live?" she haughtily responded, all but ignoring him as he watched her walk towards the bedroom door and throw it open. "This is your room isn't it?" He could feel himself losing his repose, and could not prevent his face from going dark. With eyebrows raised and his brow furrowed, he strode over to her, and with much resolve said, "It's late Annie. I need to rest." He spoke knowing that this would not be the end.

Annie moved into the room and walked over to the bed on which Millie was sitting wide-eyed and trembling with fear. "Oh! A charming domestic arrangement! How quick you have been in picking up the Jamaican ways Robert! But surely if you wanted a nigger, you could have asked me, so that I could have given you a better specimen; and I suggest you check your valuables before you turn this little slut out of here."

She turned menacingly and slammed the bedroom door to face Rutherford who still stood in the living room.

"Leave her out of it and pick on someone your own size." Before he could move however, Millie came charging out of the room, in a furious attack on Annie. The speed and temper with which she responded caught everyone by surprise.

"Slut, eh? Slut, eh? Reputation, eh? Yuh de white witch speak 'bout reputation?" The fury of Millie's attack all but bowled Annie over. Annie quickly recovered and coldly and disdainfully stepped towards Millie. "If you were one of my slaves, I would have you flogged."

"But I am not, and I am not one of your slaves, and I am not a whore, nor a tief and if de Massa...Massa seh I must stay, I will stay."

Stepping back and raising her riding crop Annie moved forward. Rutherford quickly moved between them and stopped Annie.

"If you have lost your manners, Annie, then please recover them and remember your position."

"I have constantly kept that in mind Mr. Rutherford. I am the Mistress of Rose Hall and that is my position here. I don't take insolence from field slaves; free girl indeed. I'll show a slut like you what happens to those who trespass on my estate."

Annie broke free from Rutherford's grasp and lunged at Millie, but as she raised her crop to bring it down to strike, a thunderous voice echoed from the doorway- "Mrs. Palmer!" The command in the voice had its effect and Annie turned to see Takoo standing in the doorway.

The disturbance had itself drawn other slaves including Psyche to the verandah and the windows, and they all watched as Takoo moved slowly and deliberately to his grand-daughter. "If Millie's presence caused offence I will see that she goes from here," he thundered in his deep, resonant voice.

Millie seemed to gather strength from Takoo's arrival, and spoke in a firmer tone, "Nona, Mrs. Palmer she call me whore and slut, because she jealous. Cause I love dis man."

"Love? Which whore can use love as a word?" Annie retorted in a contemptuous tone as Takoo took Millie firmly by the hand and propelled her to the door. Protesting strongly and reacting to Annie's new found onslaught, Millie heard the gasps of the onlookers and the scuffling feet as she shouted, "Fi yuh love so strong you kill three husbands, but if yuh touch my man I will see yuh dead in Montego Bay."

Annie unable to restrain herself rushed over to Millie and brought her crop down with a slashing backhand across the face of Millie, who sank moaning to the floor, blood seeping through her fingers from the cut on her face.

Rutherford guiltily rushed over and furiously grabbed the crop from Annie, jerking her forward as he broke the crop and tossed it to the corner of the room. Realizing this had gone way beyond his wildest imagination, Rutherford started across to Millie, who was already being comforted by her grandfather, who picked her up in his arms, revealing the sinewy strength which oozed from the muscles of his forearm. "This I will make you remember," he breathed quietly to Annie as he carried Millie crying hysterically to the door.

Annie hearing the onlookers chatter, shouted at him, "You don't frighten Annie Palmer — obeahman!"

Rutherford was caught in two minds, as he contemplated leaving with Millie, but decided instead to stay.

"You know what I admired about you was your poise and your dignity, but what I just saw was a vile and abominable display of crass manners."

"You poor idiotic Englishman. Are you not aware that it was Takoo who set you up with her? You really believed it was love? Did she play her part so well? Did she give you the good old black grind that turned your head?" She gave a disconcerting laugh.

Rutherford, caught somewhat off-guard, could only enquire of Annie as to why Takoo would want to set him up.

"What a fool you are Rutherford! He would set her and you up against Rose Hall. He is the only one who can do that. It suits him to have you remain as a book-keeper, where he could control you with the softness of the woman's body and prevent you from becoming the Manager of Rose Hall with Annie Palmer as your wife. Don't let them succeed in their evil plan. Come with me to the Great House."

"I would look very good in your four poster bed, wouldn't I? Rutherford, Junior book-keeper and Annie Palmer's fourth would certainly be good for your reputation — one more bought husband." Thinking he should draw her out more he asked, "And what about Ashman, you would turn him out to grass?"

"I know that you two don't really hit it off, so I would have to let him go, with good references." He knew his reply and the evening's happenings had amused to play the game, "And what if I did not love you? And said I preferred this shack?"

Smarting at the answer angrily, Annie wondered how she could put it and decided to add insult to injury, "I am aware that you show great aptitude for drinking and wenching, which covers up the ineffectual coward that you are, afraid to decide. If you had wished you could have stopped all this, if you had any form of decision in your stomach. Here I am offering you Rose Hall and instead you quiver in anticipation of a pair of soft titties — why? In two days, this field Creole has reduced you to a bowl of jelly."

Rutherford, unable to take any more, moved towards the door and with a parting shot, turned to Annie and begged to be excused. He remarked, "Far better to be a bowl of jelly than an impetuous slave owner".

Annie, her face blank, exploded with rage at the indignity of his departure, and suddenly seemed to click into motion, as she furiously formulated her next move. Having decided, she strode purposefully into Rutherford's bedroom, and opened the door to the closet, which revealed some of Millie's clothes. As the conflicting emotions played across her face, she reached out and took one of Millie's handkerchiefs and a dress and a piece of underwear, her plan now proceeding to its final stage of implementation.

Her act complete, she rode furiously back to Rose Hall, and dismounting hurriedly, rushed upstairs to her room. Her face set rigid with concentration, she changed quickly into a fresh set of dark riding clothes, and proceeded to begin the task of making a set of effigies. Before, her she placed a mug with dark liquid and began the dispensation of the libation on the two dolls. As soon as she completed the ceremony, she placed one of the effigies on her dressing table, and the other one she wrapped in what was left of Millie's garments.

Having completed her ceremony, she left her room quietly with the effigy and headed down the stairs, watched by Leila.

Annie mounted her horse and continuing her plan, set out for the mangrove swamps which lay a little away from the Great House. As she rode through the swamp, she was almost oblivious of the profusion of tropical sounds — the mass of crabs scampering from the feet of the horse and a myriad of fireflies glowing in the undergrowth.

Annie emerged out of the mangrove and moved purposefully to the village of Takoo. She stealthily dismounted and moved to Takoo's hut. When she reached the hut, she removed the effigy, and with the string attached, she suspended the effigy in a most conspicuous place, so that it would be impossible for anyone entering or leaving to miss it or not touch it with his head. Annie smiled as the effigy took on the look of a corpse dangling from a gallows.

Her task completed, she hurriedly returned to Rose Hall, feeling a mood of premonition. As she rushed up the stairs, she was in time to catch Leila in her room with the second effigy in her hand, livid with rage. She grabbed the effigy from Leila and replaced it in the drawer.

Realizing how determined Annie was, Leila fell to her knees, pleading with her in patois. But Annie merely reached down and pushed her away and out of her room.

Annie opened the drawer and removed the effigy, and sitting really still, her face rigid, a mask of total concentration, she aimed all her will power as her eyes bore into the effigy in her hand. She held a long needle, which she then plunged into the effigy. Her task complete, she collapsed in a dead faint.

As if on cue, Leila, who was waiting outside the door all the time, entered and picked her up and lovingly placed her exhausted frame on the bed.

Chapter 11

Rutherford was startled out of his sleep. He must have had a bad nightmare, but he could not shake off the feeling of impending doom, and his mind was focussed on Millie. He felt compelled to head for the compound.

He was surprised to find an air of mourning as he rode in to the compound. Sitting under a canvas which was spread to give shade to the mourning women were two drummers who were beating out a dirge used to chase evil spirits.

He dismounted and rushed into Takoo's hut, where a brazier gave off a cloud of fumes from herbs boiling in a pan placed atop the brazier — furiously Robert glowered over at Millie, and then proceeded to throw the brazier and the coal out of the window, at the same time ordering everyone in the room to leave.

Takoo, surprisingly, did not interfere, and watched as Rutherford moved over to Millie's mat. He was surprised to see how haggard and drawn she was, and the gash from the whip was vividly displayed on her drawn cheek. "What makes you think you are dying Millie?"

"She put the death curse on me last night."

"Did she come into the room?" Rutherford asked.

"No," said Millie, "but she had the spirits suck my blood."

Turning to Takoo, Rutherford said, "I hope you are listening and seeing the kind of effect your nonsense can have on the foolish and believing — you ought to be put in jail; from now on keep all your mumbo jumbo away from her.'

Takoo was about to respond, but Rutherford gave him no chance as he continued, "Millie, I want you to listen well. There are a number of things you can do to people. You can poison them, and beat them to death among other things. But you certainly can't will them to death. You are sure no one came into this room last night? Were the doors locked? And the windows? You had a nightmare Millie. I had one too, but here I am, bright and healthy and so are you.

"Take care, Robert Rutherford, take care. She will obeah you too."

"Don't be stupid and childish Millie, there is no such thing. It is just someone trying to scare you. Get up. Let me help you," but Millie shook her head weakly and called out, "Robert I don't want to die. I want to have your child."

"Then stop drivelling and get up!"

"I can't," she replied, and with that she opened her shift, and showed Robert an angry weal about the size of a shilling. "She bite me cruel, Squire."

"That could be anything, Millie — a blister, a boil. Does it hurt? I will get a doctor."

"White doctors can't help Massa Rutherford," Takoo spoke confidently.

"But witch doctors can, I suppose." Getting to his feet from beside Millie, he heard her plead for him not to go. "I am going for a doctor — that's what you need."

Bidding Takoo good day, he headed for the door, leaving Takoo raging at Annie, as to what he would do if Millie died. "I tell you white man if anything happen the white witch will die."

Rutherford took very little notice of the effigy which still dangled from the doorway until his head touched it. He ripped the effigy from its string and put it into his pocket, purposefully walking to his horse which he mounted, and without looking back, headed for town.

On his arrival, he headed for Bannion's office, and related to him the happenings of the last two days and showed him the effigy. "There isn't a doctor alive who can help," he advised Rutherford. "Nor a priest if the truth be told."

"But you don't seem to understand. There is nothing wrong with her!"

"Quite so, but if she thinks she is going to die, then she will."

"Of what Mr. Bannion? Of what?"

Bannion shrugged and spread his hands. "You don't understand Rutherford. It just happens, you once were pleased to jest about the way I cut my fingernails. I am really sorry about the girl."

"You really revolt me Bannion."

"I can only say I am sorry Mr. Rutherford."

"Who is the best doctor in the island?"

With a shrug, Bannion reached for a card and wrote Doctor Forster's address which he handed to Rutherford. "I doubt if he will bother to come. If you want my advise, you were wrong to interfere. Swallow your pride and go back to Takoo. He is the only one who can help."

"Thank you, but I thought you told me that the practice of obeah was illegal."

Robert rose from his chair as Bannion handed him back the effigy which sat on his desk during the conversation.

"Keep it Mr. Bannion. Keep it safely. You never know. It might come in useful."

As he departed, Bannion looked at the effigy and felt a sudden burst of heat. He looked up and he saw that the fan had stopped.

Robert headed for home in a violent and angry mood. On his arrival, as he entered the house, he was invited by Ryder and Burbridge to the dinner table. Not in the mood for eating, he banged the table with his fists and heatedly berated his companions for not caring. Burbridge uncomfortably replied, "You have no proof, and you are playing with fire, and the girl may recover."

He was reluctant to admit that his visit to Dr. Forster had borne no fruit, and the Doctor intimated that there was very little he could do. As if reading his mind Ryder asked, "What did Takoo think?"

"I don't know. Our parting was none too friendly," Rutherford heard himself replying.

"I don't know, but I feel he is your best bet. He could take her to one of the voodoo shrines in the hills."

"What the hell are you talking about? What is wrong with the girl?"

"Fear, Rutherford, fear, and fear is the cornerstone of faith. And I, Ryder should know, as I started out by being a priest." This disclosure surprised them all, and so forced him to tell the story of his defrocking for drink.

"It exists, my friend, it exists. As long as you believe. The doll, the libations, just like our crucifixes and the host. You are susceptible to the supernatural. And that mark on her chest? That's nothing. The girl thinks she has seen a vampire and vampires bite, and leave a mark, and if she has seen the vampire and believed — then she must have a mark. I ask you to think of miracles and the resurrection."

"To me that sounds like blasphemy."

"I would prefer to call it comparative religion," Ryder replied.

"To hell with your abstractedness Ryder. But tell me, do you believe Mrs. Palmer is a murderess?"

Looking nervously over his shoulder to see if anyone was listening, Burbridge was the first to respond, "I don't know man! And don't use that kind of language around here; you may be protected, but I need the job." He took out his watch and bade good night, as he headed for the still-house.

Turning to Ryder, Rutherford remarked, "You see he believes it, but is afraid to speak."

Ryder leaned forward, eyeing Rutherford speculatively. "You know, in addition to Takoo, there is also your tantalizing employer."

"They say she laid the curse, and I seem to feel that if she laid it, she can lift it. How the hell do I set about asking her?"

"You never know. She might be willing to strike a bargain with you. In exchange for your attendance to her bed chamber for life, she may be willing to lift the curse and let Millie live. Of course, she would not want her to live at Rose Hall."

With a glum look on his face Rutherford mulled over the words of Ryder, and deciding he had nothing to lose, he headed for Rose Hall.

His arrival was announced by William, who went upstairs to tell Annie, who with Leila, was in her room trying on some dresses she had just received that day.

"Mister Rutherford is downstairs Missus."

"Show him up William." She could see the look of disapproval on William's face, but paid no attention as she dismissed him. "At least I have something to wear," she said, as much to herself as to Leila.

As the knock on the door sounded, she invited Rutherford to enter. She saw that he was somewhat ill at ease, and turned. "Is red still considered fashionable in England? I was told that it was definitely démodé." She swirled round from the mirror to face him; and as she turned, he noticed the very low cut of the dress, and the mischievous smile on her lips.

Seeing his discomfort with Leila present, Annie excused Leila and turned her back to Rutherford once again. "Unhook me please Robert?" Reluctantly he unfastened the buttons and Annie let the dress fall to the floor, and stepping out of it, reached across for a negligeé which she draped casually around her.

"I owe you an apology, Robert. I lost my self-control last night and behaved very badly. But you are partly to blame. You must realize it is a dangerous game to keep two women at the same time, and in the same town; sooner or later it must be the cause of trouble. But I guess that's behind us now, and the slate is clean. How is she?"

"Don't you know?"

"Why should I?"

"Millie thinks she is dying and that someone has placed a curse on her."

"Oh dear Robert — you are beginning to sound like one of my slaves. Are you sure she is not suffering from some kind of guilt?"

"It's more than that. Someone has hung a toy effigy outside her hut and she believes it is you. It is so ridiculous, but now that we have wiped the slate clean, I want you to tell Millie that you were not responsible, since she seems to have taken it so seriously. Will you tell her?"

"Robert, a Negro wench publicly accuses me of murder and I am supposed to belittle myself for her? You are asking a lot, Robert."

Rising from the bed, and looking at herself in the mirror, "You know Robert, it is so difficult to keep up with fashion all this way from England."

"Annie, she is very ill. Did you not hear me?"

Paying very little attention, she continued to preen before the mirror.

Turning from the mirror, she provocatively looked at Robert, and not able to control himself any longer, he strode across the room and grabbed her by the shoulders and shook her. "I said she's dying, don't you understand?" With great effort, Rutherford controlled himself and allowed Annie to move away.

"You know Robert, you have the most curious way to ask a favour, but it's nice to see you have not entirely lost your manhood."

His eyes now wild with anger, Rutherford retorted, "You sicken me. You think you can switch off emotions as you wish, order judicious tears and 'ho-ho' off to bed and sex."

Annie smiled knowingly at Robert, and began to disrobe. She watched his body respond to the appealing display of her womanhood, and looking over at him, said, "You know Robert, perhaps we should begin Act Three, and see if we can save your Millie."

She lit the candelabra and sensuously wiggled her negligeé clad body under the bed sheets.

"I promise I will send for Takoo. Don't worry. But I didn't do it, Robert. I mean I did not, but I am beginning to be very fond of you Robert, and I must admit I am looking forward to Act Three and Act Four should be interesting, if not cataclysmic.

"But tonight, Robert, I have other things and persons to accuse me. So until I commence with Act three, I will indulge in acts of extreme pleasure and pain. Leila," she digressed, "please fetch William as I have a task for him."

Chapter 12

Rutherford left Rose Hall a little less confused than when he arrived, but was fully convinced that he had done all that was in his power to do for Millie. He arrived at his quarters an exhausted and drained man and fell immediately to sleep. He was suddenly awakened by a curious noise, and opened his eye to see Psyche leaving his room with something in her hand. Deciding not to shout at her, he dressed quickly and rushed out of the room to see Psyche moving quickly ahead.

Robert decided to awaken Ryder to accompany him and they moved swiftly after Psyche, heading towards the village. About three hundred yards from the path to the village she turned, and Robert wondered where she might be going; even more so. What could she have wanted from his room?

In the distance, however, he could hear the sound of drums. As he approached the end of the path, he saw the flickering fire and the sounds got louder. Robert could see in the distance, a simple grass hut and some fifty or so male dancers stripped to the waist, dancing with an equal number of women dressed in red. With every hypnotic beat of the drum, the dancers' eyes became more glazed.

Robert watched as Psyche now entered the circle and skirted the dancers. As she reached close to the hut, Robert saw Takoo appear. He was garbed in long red cloth, and an ornate headdress. In his hand, he carried a curious staff — the symbol of a true master of the Supernatural — Psyche curtsied and handed him the article of clothing, which Rutherford recognized was what she took from his room.

Rutherford edged closer to the action, and was startled by a tiny bag with the skull of a small animal attached to it which dangled before his face.

In the clearing, the rhythm quickened and a young girl could now be seen, foaming at the mouth and shouting incoherent words. The drumming stopped, and the dancers paused in their glazed state as Takoo approached carrying Millie in his arms. Millie was dressed in white, and a cloth was wound around her neck. Behind Takoo was a young Negro, wearing a loin cloth and leading a white goat kid.

As Takoo reached the centre of the clearing, the drums softly resumed their beat. Takoo placed Millie carefully on the ground and took the piece of cloth, the one Psyche brought, and laid it on Millie's forehead. He then took her hand and placed it on the cloth, as someone handed him his calabash.

Speaking in his vernacular and chanting, Takoo sprinkled part of the liquid on the ground next to Millie. As Millie stirred and began to be aware, no one noticed a slight figure on a horse, sitting immobile in the shadows.

Takoo having completed his prayer, reached inside his robe and produced a long sharp knife, which he held high. The blade glistened in the light, as the young boy brought forward the goat kid, with its neck stretched over a bowl, to catch the blood. With one quick move, Takoo sliced the kid's throat, and the gurgling blood filled the bowl, which he took over to Millie, and dipping his finger in the bowl, he opened the top of Millie's blouse and used his finger to circle the spot where Millie was bitten while he counted quietly in French creole. He watched as Millie seemed to revive, and her eyes open, she stared at her grandfather.

At that moment Annie, in the shadows, knew she had to make a move, and with that a piercingly loud and drawn out scream was heard, with the shout

"Erzoulie, Erzoulie!"

As if on cue, appearing among the bushes, was the grotesque and enormous figure of a bull, if one could call it a bull. It was indeed twice the natural size of any bull Robert had ever seen. Its eyes were glowing red and from its neck hung a phosphorescent chain. It pawed the ground as if preparing to charge, yet in all of this it seemed unreal and somewhat ill defined. The cries of *"Erzoulie"* continued and the bull seemed to move forward, and this forced the slaves to scatter with the shouts of "Rolling calf! Rolling calf!"

The clearing was almost empty and the outline of the beast began to fade. Takoo looking mesmerized, stooped down and picked up Millie in his arms. Facing the dying apparition—he seemed to entreat and in unintelligible mutterings pray.

The dark figure on horseback now rode into the square. Rutherford recognized it was Annie. She was alone, and looking around her, she laughed contemptuously. A second triumphant peal of laughter rang out as she circled her horse around the fire, trampling Takoo's calabash and other objects, before riding off ghostlike into the night.

Robert and Ryder turned and moved back through the undergrowth, seeking to get their breath back. All Rutherford could think of saying was, "Get Dr. Forster for Millie. I will go and deal with Madame Erzoulie." He made off in the direction of the Great House.

By the time Rutherford arrived, Annie had changed into a soft negligeé, and with its back gathered in a loose bow, looked the picture of the innocent wife, almost childlike in appearance.

Taking note of his torn clothing and dishevelled appearance Annie asked, "What's the matter darling?" Rutherford looked at her as if hypnotized, trying to balance in his mind the contrasting picture of what he had seen earlier, and its contrast with the woman he now stood before.

Seeking to control his anger he blurted out, "You lied to me Annie. You lied about Millie. You never had any intention to help."

"I tried Robert. I really tried."

"I saw it all Annie. I was in the woods. It has taken me a long time to believe all those stories I was hearing, but I have seen it with my own eyes.

"Robert, it was my duty to break up an illegal gathering."

"Break up a gathering? You practised sorcery!"

"But I had no choice, Robert. You must know that slave uprisings are triggered off by such gatherings, and my first concern must be for Rose Hall."

"I don't give a damn about Rose Hall. I want Millie to live, and unless there is a marked improvement in her condition by tomorrow evening, I will report you to the Magistrates in Montego Bay."

"You wouldn't dare!"

"I am not threatening Annie. I am telling you, and I have Ryder as a witness, so if you know what can happen, then I suggest you see that Millie makes a miraculous recovery."

Annie leaned back comfortably and looked at Robert. "If you really believe all this Robert, aren't you afraid what I can do to you? You saw what others saw, so what if I decided to visit you in your room tonight?"

"Your mumbo jumbo does not frighten me, Annie, so try another way."

"You know, Robert, one of my husbands said as much, and learnt differently."

"Takoo helped you poison them, didn't he? And if Millie dies he will turn against you and I will see to it that the cases are re-opened."

"I can't undo what's done Robert, not now, it's gone too far. I don't think anybody can.

"Try, Annie or twenty-four hours from now you will face a murder charge." Robert strode out as Annie watched him incredulously.

Rushing after him, Annie shouted, "Go to your Magistrates with your Annie tale. Do you think anyone would believe a nobody —a defrocked priest and a nigger witch-doctor over the largest plantation owner in Jamaica, and over the love of a wench slave?" Rutherford took two steps towards her as if to hit her, but controlling himself, turned and walked away.

Chapter 13

The compound was full of women wearing red, and as they moved in deep trance and sorrow, their movement was accompanied by a chant, some sat on the benches and exchanged a few words, while others watched the carpenter, making a simple coffin. Now and again, there would be a piercing cry of sorrow.

Rutherford stood near the entrance to the hut viewing the scene with apprehension. As he looked at Takoo, he looked to have aged since the night's proceedings and this seemed to have robbed him of his earlier authority. The Council of Elders, were clustered around Takoo, listless and uninspiring.

In contrast, many of the Elders and slaves were angry and Robert sensed forebodings of a serious nature, more so if the strength of leadership and direction were taken away from Takoo.

"The White Witch steal his spirit. Look at him—Takoo the King— look pon him, him favor a poor old Negro who only know fi seh 'Yes Massa' an 'No Massa'. Him can't even protect him own grandchild."

"Well old man, if Millie dead wi a go follow Aaron." Robert watched as they all moved off to leave Takoo alone.

Robert's reverie was shaken by the arrival of Ryder and Dr. Forster, and he rushed up to him with great anticipation as Millie was decidedly deteriorating. After a brief exchange, he took him in to Millie.

Dr. Forster, a tall, sharp-featured man, had spent many years in the tropics and had by now adjusted to the fact that there were certain medical happenings which took place in these parts of the world that lacked rational explanation. But as a Doctor who had taken the hippocratic oath, he at least had to go through the motions. He quickly bent down beside Millie and took her pulse and was alarmed at the very faint feel; after completing his examination, he turned to Rutherford. "Pulse very faint. I am afraid she won't last the day, Rutherford. Only a miracle... "

Rutherford, filled with rage, did not allow him to finish his sentence. "I know and that does not form a part of your bag of tricks."

Sensing the rage of Rutherford and realizing that things were beginning to escalate on the outside, Ryder took hold of Dr. Forster and ushered him outside the hut.

As they emerged, they both could sense the escalating situation; the anger of the slaves was becoming more audible. Striding purposefully and hurriedly towards his horse, Dr. Forster noticed two slaves approaching the gate. As he arrived at the gate, the slaves uncharacteristically pushed the Doctor aside, but as Dr. Forster was about to react, Ryder grabbed hold of him.

"Confound their insolence, Ryder. Are those Rose Hall men?" Ryder himself had become increasingly aware of new faces arriving at Rose Hall and was becoming more and more aware that things were getting out of hand.

"No I don't think they are, Doctor."

Dr. Forster looked intently at Ryder and felt compelled to reply, "Well, if that is so Ryder, then I would clear out of here, if I were you, as this looks a lot like serious trouble to me."

Ryder headed back to the hut. Furrows of concern, and a little fear darkened the brow of his forehead, and his eyes narrowed with the intensity of the moment. He entered the hut to see Rutherford bending close to Millie, who was now even weaker. Ryder saw the haggard look on Rutherford's face, but knowing the urgency of the situation, and sensing the increasing tempo of the drums, urged Rutherford to leave.

Rutherford shook off Ryder's urgings and decided that it was impossible for him to leave Millie — not now.

Rutherford sat patiently beside Millie, except for a brief moment when the drumming stopped, and he looked out to see that the cause was a break for eating. He was startled some hours later when Millie stirred and drifted back to consciousness. Hopefully, he moved even closer and noted a slight smile playing around her eyes. A surge of hope filled him as he reached for her hand, and whispered, "Oh Millie, you are getting better?"

Looking intensely at him, Millie whispered, "Don't let's lie to each other Squire."

"But Millie, you do know that that thing you saw is not real. There are no vampires, no rolling calves Millie I want you to live. You are not to slip away. You must live."

"Kiss me Robert." As he leaned over to kiss her on her forehead, he saw her drift off into unconsciousness.

Sensing there was very little else he could do, Rutherford rose and exited the hut. He was even more confused. He ignored the laughter of some of the women, who were still eating under the tent, and did not even take notice of the woman who entered the hut. His first recognition of this was the piercing scream that assaulted his ears, compelling him to turn and see the woman — he now realized was Psyche rushing out of the hut, her face distorted with grief, tearing at her clothes and hair. Rutherford sat resignedly and wept.

Rutherford recognized that things were moving quickly, but failed to recognize the significance of the move by one of the drummers who moved quickly across the compound to retrieve the conch shell which he furiously blew as a signal to the whole estate.

Saddened and weakened by all he had witnessed (and realizing there was very little more he could do), he mounted his horse and headed for what he sensed would not be his home for long.

Rutherford was unaware of how fast events had moved while he was at Millie's bedside.

He had yet to learn of Aaron's attack on the overseer in the field of New Hope.

The overseer, Rutherford later learned, had been trussed and dumped in the well pit and the slaves led by Aaron had taken off in the cane fields, with their machetes newly sharpened.

Meanwhile over at the boiler house, a scared Burbridge reported to Ashman who was now moving around the estate to see what was really happening.

"I don't know what's the matter with them Sir. There is a funny feeling in the air. They are working slowly. They stare back defiantly. They don't seem afraid."

"Get the overseer there and use the whips man, and keep your eyes peeled. I am going to see Mrs. Palmer."

As he moved off from the boiler house, Ashman saw the unmistakable approaching shape of Annie. He awaited her arrival, and before he could say anything, she sharply queried of him why no work was taking place over at Long Gut. Rather puzzled, Ashman reminded her that that was where Rutherford was put in charge.

"No sign of him or anyone else, so I suggest you get rid of Rutherford, and I want you to do it today and get rid of Ryder as well."

Annie could see the satisfaction on Ashman's face and reinforced her decision, "See that they get off the estate today."

"With pleasure, Annie, but please be careful — there is something very wrong." They both turned and rode off in different directions.

Burbridge turned back inside the boiler house and immediately noted the absence of any chatter; only the rumble of machinery could be detected. Out of precaution, Burbridge had himself decided to put additional overseers in place. His years of experience there had taught him to be ready for anything.

In the distance, he heard the sound of a conch shell and almost simultaneously with its sound the slaves stopped working and moved menacingly towards the overseers. Suddenly, they had weapons in their hands, and anything became a weapon — sticks, iron bars, knives, machetes.

As the slaves advanced, the overseers retreated, moving closer and closer to Burbridge, who was shouting for them to get back.

Deciding that a response was needed, an overseer raised his whip, only to be overpowered by a melee of flailing sticks, as he was hoisted and dumped into a large vat of rum. As he surfaced, spluttering, he was pushed down once again by dozens of black hands.

The slaves rushed the other two overseers and Burbridge and beat them to the ground; after the first attack, which drove him to the ground, Burbridge reached for his pistol and fired into the mob as he made a dash for the door. The shooting which had seen two men fall, temporarily halted the slaves, and allowed Burbridge to slam the heavy door shut and bolt it.

Wasting no time, Burbridge headed for the quarters.

On arrival, Rutherford found Ryder putting his last belongings into a hold all. "I used to be so glib with my condolences, Robert, but words fail me now."

"She loved me Ryder, and I failed her."

"Such is the nature of things, Robert. We invariably seem to fail each other when most in need. Here, try this shot of rum."

They both turned at the sound of galloping hoofs followed by the sharp stamp of someone ascending the verandah. The door was unceremoniously forced open by a panting Burbridge, almost completely out of breath and looking quite distraught. "Slaves rioting and killing. Warn Mrs. Palmer and Mr. Ashman. Call them and tell them I have had to run and leave the boiler house and I am gone for help." Turning sharply on his heels, he rushed off into the night.

Burbridge's arrival brought both men to life, as they sensed how serious the matter had become.

Rutherford was the first to respond, as he urged Ryder to come with him to the Great House.

"Rutherford we owe no loyalty there, and prudence to me, suggests that we head for Montego Bay."

"We can't leave her to be hacked to death by half crazed slaves. No matter what, Ryder, we must help."

"Do you have a gun, Ryder?" Ryder shook his head as Robert grabbed a whip and they both left hurriedly for Rose Hall, where Rutherford knew where the guns were stored.

Their arrival at Rose Hall was uneventful, and indeed all seemed normal. Rutherford noticed a light in Annie's bedroom; but for that the rest of the house was in darkness.

He rushed up to the steps of the main doors, which were unaccustomarily wide open, but before he mounted the steps, he saw a body appear at the window of Annie's bedroom, and with a crash the body hurtled through the window, and almost in slow motion landed at his feet, amidst shattering glass and broken window frame.

As the body thudded to the ground, a gun came clattering out of its hand and came to rest at Rutherford's feet. He recognized the body as that of Ashman, and was now more conscious of the sound of the slave riots in the distance as they came closer.

At the same time, Burbridge came thundering down the driveway but by this the slaves had extended a rope across the drive way, about horse rider height, and by the time he could see it, he was flung from his horse and some twenty slaves emerged from their hiding and with glinting machetes hacked him to death.

As in the aftermath of a battlefield, Rutherford stepped over the corpses lying on the stairs and in the hallway. He rushed up and entered Annie's room and as he entered he saw Takoo holding Annie in a stranglehold with one hand on her mouth.

Annie was struggling furiously, and his arrival with Ryder close behind surprised the slaves. One of them lunged at Rutherford and he fired, hitting him in the chest. The shot created the effect that Rutherford wished for, and with a menacing look Rutherford pointed the gun in different directions as he ordered the slaves to drop their weapons. The machetes went clattering to the floor, and turning to Takoo, he ordered him to release Annie.

Unexpectedly, he saw Takoo tighten his grip and swing Annie around so that she now shielded him with her body — "De White Witch will die white man."

"Release her Takoo. Release her, please." Rutherford realized that he had to be careful as any move in the wrong direction would mean that he could be jumped by the slaves, and Ryder was not going to be of much help in his unarmed state.

"Takoo if you harm Mrs. Palmer, you know you will hang."

From outside, Rutherford, as did Takoo, could hear the increasing ugly sounds of the rioting slaves, and in the distance the fires burning in the cane fields could be seen through the windows.

The slave noises drew closer and shouts of "Kill de white witch" could be heard. Robert knew he had to act and act quickly or he would lose any initiative he may have.

But it was Takoo who first responded. "As chief of the Negro Nation of Jamaica, I sentence her to death."

He had to act fast, Rutherford quickly responded. "You poor besotted fools, don't let Takoo talk you into the gallows. If Mrs. Palmer has broken the law, she will be punished."

"By who, white man? By your justice, the white man justice! No, I Takoo know that justice."

Rutherford heard the shouting coming even closer and decided to play his last trump card.

"If you slay her, are you not afraid of the vengeance she will take? You and yours will be cursed and haunted forever by the hosts of the spirit world, and this estate will be haunted forever, at her command."

Annie, now realizing the drift of Rutherford's approach, let her eye go rigid and her face take on a look of concentration seen only before when she drove the pin into Millie's effigy.

The slaves faltered at her look and began to back away fearfully as if an apparition were about to materialize. The tension was broken by the sound of the windows smashing and doors bursting as the roar of the mob entered the house.

Rutherford, seeking to regain the initiative, shouted, "Remember Rolling Calf! Remember Rolling Calf!" His words, however, had the opposite effect as they galvanized Takoo into action and he tightened his grip on Annie. Her choking groan moved the slaves to action, and Rutherford was able to get off just one shot before he was overpowered and held by two heavily-built slaves.

The slaves led by Aaron poured into the houses with torches in one hand and machetes and various weapons in the other.

With cries of "Where is de witch? The witch must die!" they began to smash the furniture. Takoo let go of the limp body of Annie Palmer, and she slumped to the floor. Takoo, looking exhausted, ordered the slaves to set them free. A little reluctant to move, Takoo ordered them a second time and with that they released Rutherford.

"Tomorrow white man we may have to fight you, but tonight you are free to go. We have no quarrel with you."

Takoo, moving with his recovered regal bearing, led the slaves out of Annie's room. On reaching the top of the stairs, he looked down at his followers and amidst cheers he announced, "De White Witch dead."

Back in the room Rutherford and Ryder lifted Annie's body from the floor unto her bed, standing numb with shock. They arranged Annie's hands over her body and covered her with a sheet, while Ryder, making the sign of the cross, very quietly spoke in Latin.

They both looked around the room, which was in a shambles, with side boards wrecked, curtains pulled down and armchairs hacked to pieces.

Downstairs in the Drawing Room, the scene was repeated, except that the slaves had now raised their torches to the curtains; a strange eerie glow took over the room, and the large painting of Annie which hung over the mantelpiece was dislodged and fell, and as it fell it seemed to come alive in the flickering candlelight. As the portrait was reflected in the dark windows and the mirrors, it appeared to the slaves as if Annie was on the outside wishing to come in.

Some of the slaves saw the apparition and backed away, terrified, some shouting, "De white witch come back — de white witch come back!"

Aaron, standing not too far away, turned angrily on Takoo and lunged at him with his torch. Takoo reacted and stumbled as Aaron shouted, "Old man yuh lie!" He grabbed a machete and drove it fiercely into Takoo's neck. The slaves all rushed in panic from the house, leaving the rooms burning fiercely.

Rutherford, smelling the burning curtains, picked up the body of Annie, and stepped towards the stairs. In the distance, he saw the crimson fields and in the light saw the bodies of the disappearing slaves fleeing from the house. As he descended the stairs, the landing collapsed and as if on signal, the candelabra crashed at his feet and sent showers of sparks flying, and he could swear he heard a familiar voice - but it couldn't possibly be - "I'm ready for Act IV Robert."

Rose Hall Today

oday, the restored Rose Hall stands as a testimony to Annie's life and reign; restored by John Rollins who perceived the dream of restoration and executed it, Jamaica and the world now has the opportunity to hear the story of Annie Palmer - the legend, its truth and its history. Rose Hall estate has remained in the midst of development — with new hotels and guest houses, restaurants, attractions and other resorts. In fact, the house has forced hoteliers and developers to become equipped to deal with the traffic that enters Montego Bay to simply see the Great House. Any visit to Montego Bay would be incomplete without a visit to the Rose Hall Great House. The history of the estate has shaped the current history of the city to such a great extent that it is impossible to ignore. Her story has worldwide appeal and many outside of Jamaica can recall the tales they have heard of Annie Palmer and even the Great

House, which had most of its interior decorations and paintings imported from other parts of the island and the world, is overshadowed by the cruelty of a woman schooled in black magic by a Haitian priestess.

The estate, however, has experienced much growth since the time of Annie Palmer. For example, the area now known as Rose Hall was once the entire estate of Rose Hall. Since the time off Annie Palmer, the property has been subdivided and has become land for housing development, attractions, golf courses and hotels. Many of these

developments have been indubitably marked by the existence of Annie Palmer. The attractions close to the great house permit a full day of activities while allowing a full tour of Rose Hall. For example, The *White Witch Restaurant* features local cuisine and is a stone's throw away from the Great House.

The restaurant has benefited from the intrigue created by its name and is indicative of the influence of the legend of Annie Palmer on the area. Other quality restaurants & bars can be found in the hotels surrounding the Great

House. All these restaurants reflect the pervasive influence of the white witch legend on the area; almost every one has at least one dish or drink named alluding to Annie Palmer or, her more popular name, *The White Witch*.

There are quite a number of hotels which are relatively close to the Rose Hall Great House. They include: *Wyndham Rose Hall Resort and Country Club, Half Moon Hotel* (taking its name from its perfectly shaped beach)

and the *Ritz Carlton*. Apart from helping to host patrons during popular music events (Reggae Sumfest and the Jazz festivals), they help to offer a variety to the day and night life of the area. All three hotels are golf resorts and, while maintaining high standards of quality, have managed to include the traditions of Jamaican peoples in their activities and offerings to tourists and locals alike.

Of course, the city of Montego Bay is not to be excluded. It was the home of National Hero Sam Sharpe and it was there that he led his Christmas revolt. Montego Bay at one point also boasted the island's only newspaper, Cornwall Chronicle, outside of Kingston. The city probably holds as much history as Rose Hall itself. Not far from Rose Hall, the city is the centre of major tourist and local activity and contains a number of resorts and features. The development of hotels, restaurants and sports bars along Gloucester and Kent avenues have created Mo-Bay's *hip strip*. This strip includes world famous Doctors' Cave Beach Resort, the genesis of the major developments in the city, as well as a number of new hotels, restaurants, clubs and attractions for entertainment and fine dining. Its beaches and beauty continue to rank among the best in the world. Another attraction in the city proper is Harbour Street. The local crafts market is located along Harbour Street. It is in this crafts market that you can haggle over prices or pick up authentic African-style braids and beads.

While the area has always been aware of its natural picturesque beauty, the businesses and development of the area has shown an appreciation of its own beauty and can be seen in its accentuation of its beaches, landscape, attractions and making use of its most valuable natural asset - its people.